A Thorny Past

Clara Ann Simons

A Thorny Past

A Sapphic Police Thriller

Clara Ann Simons

For more information, or to find out about new publications, please contact by email at claraannsimons@gmail.com

Twitter: @claraannsimons1

Instagram: claraannsimons

Tiktok: @claraannsimons

Index

I squirm in the backseat, every instinct screaming to run when they open the door. But that would make me a fugitive, on the run forever. I've tried so hard to leave my old life behind, even though fate keeps pulling me back into it.

The cuffs chafe my wrists. I keep my head down, an old prison habit. Avoid the guards' gazes. I hate being treated like a dangerous animal, assumed guilty by default.

Too much like those marches from cell to yard back in max security. Always watching us, controlling our every move. I swore I'd never feel that again, that I left it all behind for good.

Yet here I am, back in custody without doing anything wrong, my fragile freedom stripped away.

Chapter 2

Crow

"Keep your cool and don't cause any trouble," Detective Alvarez spits out, leaning in close enough for me to catch the mint on her breath, a stark contrast to the stale coffee aroma of the interrogation room.

I bite my tongue, literally, to keep the snark at bay. Making a scene in the middle of a police station is a game I can't win. Still, as we enter the interrogation room, even with the cuffs biting my wrists, I'm itching to headbutt her and give her pretty nose a new twist.

The light in here is unforgiving, stark fluorescence that hasn't changed since I last saw the inside of one of these rooms. It's designed to break you, to squeeze confessions out like juice from a ripe lemon.

Detective Álvarez drags a metal chair across the tiled floor. She slaps some crime scene photos on the table between us, the glossies shining under the harsh light.

"Let's make this quick, Crow. Neither of us wants to be here longer than we have to," she says, tapping a photo like she's tagging a friend in a meme. "You know this guy?"

I exhale, rolling my eyes. "Like I told you, no."

Alvarez clears her throat, flipping through the file before continuing the dance.

"About forty-eight hours ago," she begins, sliding over a police report for my perusal, "this guy was found by the canal. One bullet, back of the head—execution style."

Police Report Number 55498

On May 15th, at 10:23 pm, the Police Department received an anonymous tip about a possible homicide near the South Canal. Officers Rodriguez and Thompson were first on the scene at 10:37 pm.

Upon arrival, they discovered the lifeless body of a Hispanic male, sprawled on his back near the water's edge. A single gunshot wound to the back of his head, point-blank range. No weapon, no casing found.

The scene was secured for the forensic team, and the investigation commenced.

The victim was identified as Diego Ortega, 32. No ID on him, but fingerprints got us a name.

Preliminary forensic reports peg the cause of death as the gunshot wound to the head, death on impact. Powder burns around the wound, but no other visible injuries.

The scene whispers 'homicide,' given the wound and the circumstances. Considering the guy's criminal record, a revenge hit isn't off the table.

Officer James Rodriguez

Badge Number 45632

May 15th, 2024

"Wow, you're telling me the evidence points to homicide?" I chuckle, my voice dripping with sarcasm. "Even a toddler could've called that one, detective."

Isabella doesn't crack a smile. "Cut the act, Crow," she says, her finger landing on one of the glossy photos spread between us. Despite my resistance, my gaze shifts.

The lifeless stare of the man in the photograph locks onto mine, his terror frozen in time. Blood and brain matter paint a grisly abstract on the grimy pavement behind him. Yet, it's not the fatal wound that draws me in—it's the black rose nestled against his cheek, almost lovingly placed, that I know all too well.

"A Black Baccara," I whisper, nudging the photo closer to Detective Alvarez.

"Your calling card. That's why I'm here with you instead of enjoying my Friday night."

"With your sunny disposition?" I mutter, my words barely above a breath. "Do you really think I did this?"

"Let's just say you're currently... interesting to this case. Your history is hard to overlook. So, where were you that night?"

"The night of Wednesday?" I smirk, leaning back in my chair. "In my apartment, busy with... personal engagements. You know, fucking."

"I'm guessing you're not lucky enough to have a witness willing to vouch for that? That lucky girl, maybe?" she presses, her eyebrows lifting in a challenge.

"I doubt she'd volunteer to walk into a police station." I cross my arms defensively. "Go ahead, search my place. Don't even bother with a warrant."

"Crow," she starts, and there's a flicker of something almost like respect in her eyes, "I'm going to give you the benefit of the doubt—for now. Someone might be mimicking your old ways. Who else knows about the roses?"

I can't help but roll my eyes.

"After the fame you brought me eight years ago? Let's just say, my dance card's been full since."

"I assume you don't grow them anymore."

"You're about eight years too late, Alvarez."

"The forensic team found something on two petals and the stem," she continues, locking her gaze with mine. "Traces of ambergris."

"Should that ring a bell?"

"It's a substance from sperm whales, can fetch up to $80,000 a kilo," she explains, matter-of-fact.

13

"That's a very expensive fertilizer for a black rose."

"It's used in high-end cosmetics. Perfumes, mostly. Whoever left that rose wears a scent worth hundreds," she says, leaning back and stretching her arms above her head.

"Detective, in my current state of affairs, I'm lucky if I can afford off-brand deodorant," I grumble, still baffled at how this woman caught me eight years ago if her smarts are half-baked. "I highly doubt I fit the profile of someone draped in hundred-dollar perfume."

"Maybe you stole it," Isabella suggests.

"Yeah, right. Because I've got nothing better to do than risk another stint in the slammer for a bottle of scent," I retort, clicking my tongue in disdain and rolling my eyes for effect.

"I'm just following the evidence," she defends herself with a shrug.

"You're following it the wrong way. Look at the crime scene. The rose, it's placed so deliberately, almost like it's part of the blood-splattered set design." I lean forward, eager to paint the picture for her. "That, and the pricey perfume, it tells us our perp's got a taste for the finer things: luxury, beauty. It's all intentional," I explain, my voice a mix of exasperation and sarcasm.

"Again, you're fitting the bill."

"Shit! Let me see the photo!"

"This one?"

"In digital, do you have it in digital? I need a closer look," I insist, my curiosity piqued by something that caught my eye.

Detective Alvarez makes a move to stand up but then quickly settles back down, shaking her head and raising her hands in a no-go.

"Ah, no, no. You're not touching a computer. Who knows what you could pull off with one of those hooked up to the police's network."

"I haven't hacked anything in eight years, Alvarez. Tech's moved on without me." I'm almost pleading now, just wanting a closer look at what I've seen.

After a moment's hesitation and a heavy sigh, she signals one of her colleagues through the one-way mirror across from us. Soon enough, another officer enters with a tablet loaded with case photos.

"Do you guys actually fool anyone with those mirrors?" I can't help but ask, with a sly grin.

"Focus, Crow! Don't waste my time," she barks.

"Zoom in right there. Look, see that bracelet on the ground? Just outside the secured area? It's easily worth north of twelve grand. Did you guys pick it up as evidence?" I point out, my finger hovering over the silver glint partially hidden in the grass.

Detective Alvarez's face loses color as she realizes the oversight of her team. She looks at me, her mouth opening and closing a couple of times, but the words, they just don't come out.

"Unbelievable, seriously!" I blurt out, slapping my forehead, but I'm quick to add, "I mean that in the most respectful way possible, Detective." I pause, considering whether it's even worth it to revisit the scene. "Because whoever stumbled upon that bracelet lying on the ground hit the jackpot, considering it could've led you straight to your killer. But hey, that bracelet's only sold in two shops in this city, so good luck to the lucky finder!"

"And how would you know that?" she asks, her eyebrow arched in suspicion.

I lean back, holding up my hands like I'm surrendering, "I got offered a job to hit one of those stores three weeks back. Swear to God, I turned it down. I don't want any part of that life anymore," I say, nodding towards the handcuffs still circling my wrists.

Detective Alvarez storms out of the interrogation room like a whirlwind, and even through the wall, her voice cuts through as she rips into the officers who botched the crime scene containment.

"You know, maybe you should let me help with the case. No charge—though I wouldn't say no to a paycheck..." I trail off, and she shoots me a look.

"I thought you didn't want anything to do with the cops. Isn't that why you bolted?"

"That was before I knew there was a killer out there leaving behind the same brand of roses I used eight years ago. Either you solve this, or I'm looking at a one-way ticket back to prison, only with a much longer stay," I say, shaking my head slowly.

"You don't think we'll catch them?"

"Honestly? No."

Detective Alvarez leans in, her voice low and deliberate, each word a chisel shaping the cold air between us. "I'd rather lose a finger than work with you." Then, softer, she adds, "Get out, and don't go far. Something tells me we'll be seeing each other again real soon, Crow."

"It's Angie, by the way. I'm not Crow anymore," I murmur, pushing the door open, letting the New York chill wrap around me as I step out into the wild uncertainty.

Chapter 3

Isabella

Alone in my office, the case file open in front of me for the umpteenth time, I can't shake thoughts of Crow. Her undeniable beauty, wild and dangerous, hits me just like it did eight years ago.

It's an irrational feeling. She's a criminal of the worst kind. A thief, a hacker, who knows what else. Yet those piercing blue eyes, that untamed spirit... damn, they're hard to ignore. I'd like to think her time behind bars changed her, but experience tells me people like her rarely do.

Capturing her years ago was a nightmare. Always one step behind. I remember I even dreamt of her, a tangled web of contempt and admiration.

The scent of luxury assaults me as I step into the exclusive boutique linked to the perfume our killer used, and maybe the bracelet too.

A silver-haired man in his sixties, impeccably dressed, greets me. He sizes me up with an inquisitive look, trying to gauge if I'm here to buy or just browse. I can't help but smile at the irony. I'm on the hunt for a killer who splurges half my salary on a fragrance... or several months' worth on a bracelet.

"Looking for something in particular?" he asks, voice low, adjusting his tie.

"Detective Isabella Alvarez, Homicides," I introduce myself, flashing my badge. "I need to ask you some questions."

The man doesn't bother hiding his annoyance. He raises an eyebrow with surgical precision, as if to say he's above this, above me.

"What about?" he finally asks. "I'm quite busy this morning," he adds.

I glance around. Not a customer in sight. Given the price tags here, I doubt he's ever really busy. Only the elite few could afford these luxuries.

"I'm interested in a white gold men's bracelet with diamonds from a well-known French brand," I start, leaning casually against the glass counter. "But I'm more interested in who bought it."

The shopkeeper, all tailored suit and condescension, gives me a thin-lipped smile. "I'm always ready to assist the police, Detective Alvarez. But please understand, we cater to a very select clientele who—"

"Do you recognize this bracelet?" I cut in, sliding an enlarged photo across the counter.

He hesitates, then, "Ah..."

"Ah, what? Does it ring a bell or not?" I press.

"This case is... different. Very different," he admits, one eyebrow arched as he peers at the photo. "The man who bought it was not our usual type of client."

"What do you mean?" I prod, leaning in.

"Our customers possess a certain *je ne sais quoi*, an elegance that money can't buy. That man was quite the opposite—far from it, no matter how much he was willing to spend."

"Could you please be clear?" I demand, my patience wearing thin.

"His appearance was less than elegant—dangerous, even. He looked more like a thug than a *connoisseur*, devoid of any refinement."

"Can you describe him? Was he tall? What was his hairstyle?"

"Very tall. I'd say about six-foot-three of pure muscle. Shaved head. Not the kind of man you overlook, especially not in a store like this," he explains, tongue clicking with disdain. "Perhaps most striking was a massive snake tattoo starting below his ear, winding down his neck and part of his head. And that gaudy gold pinky ring—utterly tasteless."

"I'm guessing you don't have more details. Name, address? I guess he didn't use a credit card?"

"No, cash. Twelve thousand dollars in bills. Can you imagine, detective?"

"What I'm trying to imagine is why you didn't take down his information," I cut, upset. "You do know you're required by law to report any cash transactions over ten thousand dollars to the IRS."

He sighs, long and heavy, as if the weight of the world—or federal laws—suddenly rests on his shoulders. "It was a busy morning, detective. I barely had time for anything," he stammers out an excuse. "By the time I realized, he had already left."

"Why am I not surprised? How long ago was this? Do you remember?" I ask, trying to keep him focused.

"About fifteen days ago. A man like that doesn't fade into the background. I breathed easier the moment he left the boutique."

***

I storm back to the police station, my frustration boiling over. If that boutique idiot had done his job, we might have the killer's info by now or, at least, a nice lead. I was banking on his description to ID the guy, but either he's fresh ink or the best at playing hide and seek - because no one in our database matches the tatted-up brute.

But, honestly? My annoyance at the boutique fiasco pales in comparison to the fury that flares up when Chief Davis calls me into his office.

"I'm not working with that criminal," I spit out, raising my voice more than necessary.

Chief Davis doesn't even flinch. He lifts his gaze from his desk slowly, a stone-cold stare settling on me. "It's not a request, Detective Alvarez. It's an order."

"She just got out of prison after eight years. We don't even know if she's linked to the murder — but it's got her signature all over it," I argue, slapping the desk with both hands, drawing a lethal look from my boss.

"That woman has the most to gain from solving this murder — or the most to lose. If she's involved, it's better to keep her close. I'd rather think she believes we trust her than have her lurking somewhere we can't find her. Remember, Crow can live completely off the grid."

"Chief, you can't trust her. I know her, and—"

"Enough, Alvarez!" he barks, standing up so fast his chair rolls back with a thud.

"But, Sir—"

"It's an order, detective. Either follow it or hand in your badge and gun right now. Just keep that woman on a tight leash to prevent any more headaches."

"Incredible," I mutter to myself.

I clench my fists, the urge to punch something almost overwhelming, but then Chief snaps me back to reality. "Call her, Alvarez! And find that killer fast. Now, move!"

This is a mistake. I can feel it. Chief Davis is making a huge blunder, oblivious to just how dangerous Crow really is. She doesn't know her like I do.

If Crow's mixed up in the murder, or even if one of her buddies is, she could sabotage the whole investigation, and we'd be none the wiser.

And let's not even talk about the chance of her getting her hands on the police database. Sure, she claims she's been hacking-free for eight years, but some things never change.

Chapter 4

Crow

The ring of my phone slices through the aroma of my third morning coffee, and for some reason, a goofy grin dances on my lips as I check the caller ID.

"Detective Isabella Alvarez, you really gotta quit calling me so much. People will start talking," I tease, the words rolling off my tongue with a playful lilt.

The first thing that greets me is a sigh, heavy with frustration. This woman seriously lacks a funny bone.

"Can you not, Crow? I need to have a serious conversation with you," insists the detective, her tone all no-nonsense. "Where are you?"

"In my apartment," I quip, a smirk in my voice. "I'd send you a picture, but I'm not exactly dressed for the camera."

Isabella chooses to glide right over my bait, not giving me the satisfaction.

"I need you to come to the police station."

"With a lawyer?"

"No, as a consultant for the department," she says, and I can almost hear the blush of embarrassment staining her words.

"Could you run that by me again? I'm not sure I caught that right. You need my help?" I can't help the incredulity lacing my voice.

"It's orders from Chief Davis. If it were up to me, I'd never see you again," she growls, and I can almost picture her gritting her teeth.

"So your boss is making you team up with me? Am I getting paid for this?"

"Crow, I'm giving you twenty minutes to show up at the damn police station," Isabella insists, enunciating each syllable as if she's talking to someone hard of hearing—or an idiot.

***

"You've got a stack of paperwork to wade through before you can start working as a consultant," Isabella drawls, sliding the stack of papers across the table with a flick of her wrist that reeks of reluctance.

I arch an eyebrow at her, "Feeling tense, Detective?"

Without missing a beat, I scrawl my signature across the non-disclosure agreement, not even pretending to scan the legal terms.

"I don't usually do tag-teams with criminals," she snaps back, the word 'criminal' coming out like sour milk.

"Ex-criminal," I correct her with a smirk, leaning back in my chair, "Reformed citizen now. Even moonlighting with the cops."

She lets out another one of those long, suffering sighs that I'm beginning to enjoy way too much.

I feign a stretch, my hands inching towards her pristine desk, angling to prop my feet up.

"Don't even think about it," she warns, pointing a pen at me like it's a loaded gun.

I can't resist, "Isn't this the part where we kick back and munch on donuts? I've seen the movies, detective."

She rolls her eyes, choosing to ignore my jab as she busies herself straightening papers that don't need straightening. I decide to turn the screw, "So, Izzy. I can call you Izzy, right? Now that we're teammates, partners in crime-fighting."

"It's Detective Alvarez," she corrects firmly, "And let me lay it out straight for you. We're not partners, not friends, not anything of the sort. You're here because Chief Davis says so, and you don't do anything; don't touch anything without running it by me."

"You're less fun than my parole officer," I grumble, feigning disappointment.

"Got it, or not?"

"Yeah, yeah, fine," I wave her off, "Can't touch a computer, can't talk to my old crew, can't whisper a word about the case. Shadowed at all times in the station, at a crime scene, even in the forensics lab. What about the bathroom—do I get an escort there, too?"

"This isn't a game, Crow," she says, her voice a steel thread.

I lean in, dropping my voice to a conspiratorial whisper, "Still boxing, detective? You're looking better than you did eight years ago," I say, winking to soften the jab.

She ignores me again, but I catch that tell-tale blush creeping up her cheeks. It gives her a look that's somewhere between fierce and shy, and it's a combination I find more intriguing than I should.

"Let's start with the case," she says, all business now. "We've got a murder with your signature all over it. We're going to operate under the assumption you didn't do it. Who's mad enough at you to frame you?"

"I don't have enemies," I say quickly, maybe too quickly.

"You're not short on enemies," the detective mutters under her breath.

"Okay, maybe a few," I concede.

"Let's cut to the chase, Crow," Isabella leans in, her eyes narrowing. "Here's what I'm thinking. You've gone back to your old ways, doing what comes naturally to you. This time, things got out of hand, and that man ended up dead. How he's connected to you, I don't know— maybe a competitor, a client for your stolen goods or data?"

"So, I'm working with you guys to catch myself? That's a new one," I retort.

"You're collaborating because it's the safest bet for you," Alvarez continues, undeterred. "You think you'll have the inside track on the investigation, maybe even toy with the idea of steering it somewhere convenient. And I'll tell you why I suspect that."

"Because of the black rose?" I interject, raising an eyebrow.

"No," she replies, and there's that flicker of fire in her eyes that says she's onto something. "You're so self-centered that you can't help but leave your signature on every crime. Still, you're right; anyone could've dropped a rose to frame you. Instead, you leave a pricey men's bracelet near the crime scene—a clear attempt to throw us off. You figured if we start looking for a man, the trail goes cold on you. Am I getting close?" She points that pen at me again, and I have to admit, it's a little thrilling.

"Honey, either you watch too many movies, or you're too good at chess," I say, flashing her my best grin.

On the inside, though, my stomach's doing somersaults. Whoever did this really nailed what the detective would think. The snake tattoo doesn't ring a bell, but I'm not loving the description. I'd rather not bump into that guy.

"I have no idea what you're talking about," I mutter, straining to keep my cool. "There are certain lines I don't cross, not now, not eight years ago. I'm into theft, especially data. I don't kill, kidnap, or torture. You get me, right? And I'll do you one better. Most of my victims had it coming; they deserved it, and the money ended up in better hands."

28

"Right, like Robin Hood," she quips.

"Is that a new hacker? Nah, seriously, I know who he is. Had plenty of time to read in prison. Time stands still in that place, you know?"

"I heard you kept pretty busy; let's just say you were... quite popular among the inmates," she suddenly says, and there's that blush again.

"If I didn't know you better, I'd say you're getting jealous, Alvarez," I joke, but I'm curious about that rush of color to her cheeks.

"You haven't said anything about my theory," Isabella probes, leaning back in her chair with a scrutiny that seems to cut through the stale precinct air. "You found that bracelet when it was nothing more than a blurry smudge in a photo, as if you knew exactly where it was. My other agents missed it."

"Do you want my professional opinion on your agents?" I say, the sarcasm dripping from every syllable. "Seriously, detective, I've done my eight years. I'm out now. Do you really think I'm itching to go back? Hell, I'm on parole; one slip and it's straight back behind bars. I'm not that person anymore," I assure her, with a seriousness that surprises even me.

Isabella is about to retort when a knock at her office door cuts her off.

"What do you want, McGrath?" she barks, clearly irked.

"You need to see this, boss. Another murder, another one of those roses," the officer says, handing over a stack of papers and looking at me with disdain.

"Shit," Isabella sighs after scanning the documents, sliding them across the table so I can get a peek.

Police Report number 64278

Date: May 18th

Time: 10:45 AM.

Officer: John Waltom.

Badge number 4567

Incident Description:

At approximately 10:20 AM, a 911 call reported a motionless body in an alley behind The Iron Horse on 54th and Eighth. My partner, Officer Ramirez, and I arrived at the scene to find the lifeless body of a man, face-down on the pavement.

The victim is a Caucasian male, roughly 35-40 years old, slender build, about six feet tall, with short brown hair. He was dressed in a black suit, white shirt, and red tie. Unidentified.

An initial examination of the scene revealed a single gunshot wound to the back of the head, with an exit wound at the front. No shell casings were found, but the entry wound suggests a close-range shot with a 9mm Parabellum.

Near the right side of the victim's neck, a black rose was found.

No signs of struggle or fight. The alley has no surveillance cameras.

The scene was cordoned off, and a forensic team has been requested for evidence collection and analysis.

"The forensic team's at the crime scene now, boss," the officer announces.

"Let's go," Isabella commands, rising swiftly to snatch her coat. "And don't you dare touch anything when we get there," she warns, halting abruptly in front of me.

"I know, I know," I quip, "you're dying to slap the cuffs on me. And I'm dying for you to do it, but preferably to the headboard." I send her a wink so charged it could start a fire, earning me a lethal glare from the detective.

Chapter 5

Isabella

The familiar metallic tang of freshly spilled blood hits me the moment we step onto the crime scene, an unmistakably sharp scent, a blend of raw flesh and rust that seems to cling to everything. "Just another day at the office," I mutter to myself.

We duck under the yellow tape that marks the perimeter, and I catch a glimpse of Crow out of the corner of my eye. If I didn't know her better, I'd swear she looks out of place.

"If you so much as touch anything or pick up any evidence, I'll shoot you myself. Then I'll deal with Internal Affairs," I threaten before she can get any closer to the body.

"Your obedient 'girl scout,' detective," she quips with a mock salute that's so exaggerated it's almost comical. "Always following your lead, hands off, mouth shut—unless you say otherwise."

I roll my eyes, choosing to ignore her theatricals as the forensic team leader strides over to us. Gary's a wise old bird, on the brink of retirement, but sharp as a tack. I like working with him.

"Think you'll be interested in a couple of things," he says, nodding me toward the victim.

"What've you got?"

"It's a Caucasian male, looks about 35-40. Criminal record, like the last one. Single gunshot wound to the back of the head. Point-blank. Same as the other guy," he adds, squatting beside the corpse.

"Any other similarities?"

"You'd finish quicker by asking if there's anything different. No shell casing, no sign of a struggle. And there's your black rose," he nods, chin pointing out a perfectly placed Black Baccara beside the victim's neck—Crow's favorite.

I let out a long sigh; this is getting to be too much. Out of the corner of my eye, I see Crow inching closer.

"Here to admire your handiwork?"

"Just admiring the forensic team's handiwork," she retorts, her face unreadable.

"I suppose you've never seen this guy before either," I say, gesturing toward the dead man.

"Nope."

Her response is what I expected, but I can tell—she's not comfortable.

"There's something else you should see, Isabella," Gary interrupts, holding up a clear bag with a crumpled paper inside. "Found it in the guy's mouth. There's a message on it."

"A message?" I ask, perplexed, my curiosity piqued.

"The black rose will wither behind bars," I read out loud, the words hanging in the tension-filled air. "Does that mean anything to you?"

Crow edges closer, her eyes darting to the note with feigned nonchalance, as if she's dying to scrutinize the handwriting but wouldn't dare ask.

"You think you're being funny with these wild goose chases?" I say, my patience wearing thin. "It's getting old."

She's clearly rattled, the mask of cool indifference slipping. Shoulders tensed, her right hand balling into a tight fist, she's a coil ready to snap.

"I've told you, I'm not behind this. Can I wait in the car or something?" Her voice is clipped, probably eager to escape the crime scene that's become all too familiar.

"In the back of the squad car, Crow," I warn her, my tone steady.

She tosses a sarcastic salute over her shoulder, "Wasn't planning on boosting a cop car, they have terrible resale value," and then she's walking away.

A nagging thought tugs at the edge of my mind – maybe, just maybe, Crow's innocent. Someone could be framing her, right? But back-to-back murders fresh out of jail? That's overkill, even for her. She's flirting with a one-way ticket back to prison, and that's not her style.

One thing's for sure, she's holding back on me — I can feel it. And this second murder? It won't be the last.

"Any prints on the note?"

"Zilch. Our killer's no amateur," the forensic chief admits, almost impressed.

My phone vibrates, jolting me back to reality. My heart does a somersault as I see the name on the screen.

Crow: I need to talk to you. Urgent.

I mumble an apology, ask Gary to keep me posted, and almost sprint to where Crow has caged herself in the back of my patrol car.

"What's so urgent? Ready to confess?" I ask, half-expecting another round of her signature sarcasm.

"I need your help," she says, and there's no hint of irony in her voice now.

I'm speechless for a second. Her gaze is heavy with an emotion that feels like sorrow, distance — it's not the Crow that drives me up the wall. She looks... damn, almost vulnerable.

"My help?"

"Please, Isabella."

"You've never called me Isabella before," I sigh, unable to hide my surprise.

"I need your help," she repeats, her voice a mere whisper as if it's a secret for us alone.

"What do you need, Crow?"

"Access to a high-powered computer. I'm talking about the cybercrime unit's network."

"Fuck! You've got to be kidding me," I burst out, throwing my hands in the air in exasperation. "For a second there, you almost had me. If I let you anywhere near those computers, I can't even imagine the chaos you'd unleash. You're out of your mind if you think—"

"I know," she cuts in, urgency lacing her voice, "Please." She thrusts her cell phone at me, and the message on the screen feels like a punch to the gut.

"Now I know you're the guilty one, and you will pay for it. You can't hide from me. I've tracked every step you've taken since you got out of prison. Tick tock, tick tock. Your time is running out, Crow. Enjoy your freedom while you can because you'll soon be back in your cage."

I roll my eyes. "Laying it on thick with the drama, aren't you, Crow?"

"It's not just the message. There's an encrypted part. That's why I need the cyber unit's network," she says, pointing to a string of incomprehensible characters on the screen.

"Okay, let's say I buy your story. Let's pretend I believe you're not behind the murders but just another target. Clearly, someone's going to great lengths to set you up. They must really hate you. If I get you to that network, can you trace the phone that sent this?"

"I doubt it," she admits without missing a beat.

"Then what good will it do?"

"He wants us to decode the encrypted message. That's why he sent it."

"Wouldn't it be easier to send it unencrypted?" I ask, still not getting the full picture.

"People are weird," she shrugs. "Maybe he just wants to buy time. I don't know, but he sent this message to be read. That much I'm sure of."

Every cop instinct in me is screaming that she's trying to play me somehow, but damn it, that flicker of vulnerability in her eyes disarms me.

"Alright, we'll go," I relent, feeling my resolve crumble.

Chapter 6

Crow

Reluctantly, Detective Alvarez agrees to haul my phone over to the cybercrimes department, muttering under her breath about how I better not touch anything without her say-so. As we weave through the maze of the police station, she keeps shooting me these looks like I'm about to bolt or something.

"Meet Shelly Lorenz, head of cybercrimes," Isabella introduces, nodding towards a woman who's roughly my age, her hair pulled back in a ponytail.

"Pleasure," I say, reaching out to shake her hand.

"Wow, the infamous Crow in the flesh. I'm a huge fan. I've spent hours dissecting your ghost code algorithm. It's the stuff of legends," she gushes, her grip firm. "How did you even come up with the idea to create an encrypted communication protocol with multiple proxy nodes, each with its own unique symmetric key? Then, mix it with a one-time password system generated through hash functions, where each password expires as soon as it's used? It had our department running in circles for years," she admits, nodding with genuine respect.

Before I can dive into how my brainchild was inspired by the Dark Web's encryption systems, Isabella cuts in, "Let's keep it focused, Shelly. Crow's ego is inflated enough without you adding air."

Shelly shrugs, gives me a look that screams, "I know, Isabella can be a bit too much," and leads me to a workstation decked out with every hacker's dream: keyloggers, sniffers, exploits, RATs, rootkits, botnets. Man, I'd kill for some alone time here.

"I'm not sure it's wise to let her near a computer, Shelly," Isabella cautions as I sit down.

While Shelly's raving about the latest upgrades to a well-known hacking suite, I'm already tunneling through their network, decrypting the message. Just as I expected, it doesn't take long. Either the sender wanted us to crack it, or they're not as savvy as they think. Or both.

"What the hell is this?" Isabella blurts out, peering over my shoulder.

"Looks like some sort of riddle," confirms the cybercrimes director.

To them, it might just be a cryptic puzzle, but to me, it's a screaming warning as clear as day.

"Under the roof where the young raven first spread her wings, the little birds wait for their forgotten queen. Where her flight began, there waits the one who stole her heart. In that haven of youthful love, hides the keeper of obsession's secrets. 34.2367° N, 49.987° W. The coordinates unerringly point to where her old flame lies, near that hard-to-forget center, awaits the ghost of an innocent I'm about to kill."

"Son of a bitch," I mutter, slamming my fist on the table.

"Does this mean something to you?"

"We need to go now, Isabella," I urge, practically leaping from my chair.

"Go where?"

"It's the community center where I learned to code. They take in kids from broken homes or the streets and teach them to... well, it doesn't matter. I'll explain on the way. Let's move!"

"Shelly, not a word of this to anyone," Isabella warns sternly. "We don't know how many people are involved."

"You know you can count on me," the tech whiz assures us. "And, Crow? If you're looking for a job after you're done hanging out with buzzkill Isabella, you've got an open invitation here."

I barely have time to thank her before Isabella rolls her eyes and practically drags me out of the lab.

In the car, on our way to the community center, a heavy silence settles between us, only broken by the occasional crackle of the police radio spitting out codes and messages. It's clear now, whoever this jerk is, they're coming straight for me. No doubt about it. But it's gotten way too personal. The two victims? Just acquaintances, people I'd crossed paths with on odd jobs. They were just a warning shot.

"Now he's out to really hurt me," I muse aloud, the words hanging in the car like a challenge.

**

The moment the center's director spots me, her eyes go wide as saucers, and she wraps me in a hug that feels like it might last forever.

"You're still in one piece," she sighs, pulling back for a moment only to pull me in again.

She leads us to her office, and as we walk, I can't help but notice the old classrooms. They're just as I remember, though thankfully, the computers have seen a serious upgrade.

"We've been in a bit of a rough spot," she apologizes, catching me eyeing a wall where the paint is starting to peel. "Ever since you stopped being able to send money, things have gotten tougher. You wouldn't believe how many kids you've helped over the years, Crow," she whispers, her touch on my arm bringing back a warmth I'd almost forgotten.

Detective Alvarez tries to get some info out of the director. Still, all she manages to do is put her on edge, and that's saying something for a woman who isn't easily spooked.

"Crow, this is serious. I'm starting to believe you're not involved because none of this makes any sense if it's you. So, you're the one who needs this killer caught the most," she lays it out. "I need the names of anyone you've had... encounters with here. It's clear he's targeting one of them."

"It would take at least three hours, detective," I joke, earning me a glare.

41

"Crow..."

"There's only one name," I finally admit with a heavy sigh. "Marla Trenton."

Chapter 7

Isabella

We drive to Marla Trenton's apartment in silence, thick enough to slice through. Crow's lost in her own world, staring out the window as if the rundown streets hold some kind of fascinating secret. She doesn't bother with my attempts at conversation, her jaw set tight, probably replaying some memory.

"Marla was my first love," she finally says, her eyes never leaving the view. "I was sixteen. It might sound trivial to you, but she was everything to me at the time."

Her voice carries a heavy dose of nostalgia. Even through her reflection in the window, I swear I can see her eyes glisten. The Crow I know, all sarcasm and provocation, seems miles away.

"She was perfect, you know? Funny, brilliant. She saw something in me that no one else could see, not even myself. Made me feel valued, not like some doomed street rat. I adored her," she confesses, looking down. "Now, that son of a bitch is after her. She's the next target. If anything happens to her because of me, I'll never forgive myself," she adds, her hands balling into fists.

She pauses, blinking rapidly before turning to me with a vulnerability I've never seen in her before.

"I'll do anything to keep her safe. If that monster hurts her because of me..."

Her voice trails off, and she lets out a long sigh, turning her gaze away to hide her moist eyes. Before I know it, I find myself reaching out, squeezing her hand reassuringly.

"We'll get there first. Don't worry," I promise her.

"He sent that encrypted message not because it was hard, but to buy time, knowing he'd get ahead," she says through gritted teeth, her tough facade snapping back into place, though she doesn't pull her hand away.

Fate has us pulling up right in front of Marla Trenton's apartment complex just as she's getting back from the grocery store. Crow is out of the car before we've fully stopped, their eyes meeting in a stunned silence, like they've both seen a ghost.

"Angie?" Marla drops her grocery bags to the ground, astonished.

"It's been too long," Crow breathes out, and for a moment, they hesitate before embracing each other tightly.

"There's no time for hellos now. You'll have plenty of time to catch up later," I interject. "Ms. Trenton, these officers are here to take you somewhere safe."

She nods, her eyes still locked on Crow as she walks away with the patrol officers who've come as backup.

"I want four of you to secure the perimeter. If that bastard is in the building, we can't let him slip away," I command the officers, who immediately take their positions. "Marla will be okay, Crow. You can go with her if you want; leave this to us," I whisper, giving her shoulder a gentle squeeze.

"I'm staying with you," she declares.

I roll my eyes and ask for a bulletproof vest. There's no time for arguments, and I know she can be as stubborn as a mule when she cares about something.

Guns raised, we cautiously ascend the apartment building's stairs, which reek of grime. As we move, I sense the prying eyes of tenants peeking through their peepholes — a common occurrence here. Everyone watches, but no one ever knows or says anything. Crow takes her position behind me, while one of my officers brings up the rear, guarding against any surprise attacks from behind.

I raise a clenched fist to halt us, then tap my ear repeatedly with two fingers, signaling them to listen for any sounds. Just as I'm about to give the command to move on, I hear someone running. He's sprung from nowhere, leaping with the prowess of an Olympic athlete.

"Stop, police!" I shout, aiming my gun, but he's already sprinting down the stairs, unaware that two of my men are waiting for him at the entrance.

A brief scuffle ensues, and within moments, I get a radio message confirming they've got him.

"Let's check the apartment," I suggest in a low voice, nodding for us to enter. It seems, for once, luck is on our side.

"Freeze!" I suddenly hear.

Crow grabs me around the waist and pulls me back, throwing us both to the ground and sticking close to me.

"What the hell are you doing?" I protest, gasping for air, and the warmth of her body against mine is an odd sensation.

"Look, on the floor, about six inches ahead," she points out.

Fuck, if my heart was racing before, now it's practically stopped. I freeze, a cold sweat breaking out on my forehead as I contemplate the implications. Right behind the entrance, barely visible, someone has stretched a thin nylon wire.

"It's a trap," Crow whispers right next to my ear, still glued to me as if I wasn't fully aware she probably just saved my life.

"Crow, where the hell are you going?" I protest as she gets up and moves into the apartment, skillfully avoiding the tripwire at the entrance.

She cautiously follows the trail until she abruptly stops, shaking her head and looking back at us.

"Bomb, get out of here!" she yells, motioning with her hand for us to leave.

"Call dispatch, get a bomb squad here, now!" I bark at the officer with us, who's turned pale as a ghost. "Don't just stand there like an idiot; we need to start evacuating the building."

"There's no time," Crow sighs, her voice eerily calm, before she bends down to inspect the bomb.

I stand a few feet away, unsure how to react. The officer with us sprints down the stairs as if the devil himself was on his heels.

Our eyes meet, and when she pierces me with those determined blue eyes, something clicks in my head. Despite all my efforts to resist, in this moment, I'm ready to trust her with my life. For better or worse, right now, our lives are hanging by the same thread.

"Crow, please tell me you know what you're doing," I whisper, on the verge of panic.

She just ignores me, tilting her head to examine the bomb from different angles, gently tracing the wires with her fingertips, her brow furrowed.

Before I know it, she grabs a wire and pulls it sharply. Instinctively, I close my eyes and cover my face with my arms as if that could save me if the bomb were to explode.

"You can look now, detective," Crow hisses, her breath still ragged.

"Holy shit," I mutter, wiping the sweat off my forehead with my jacket sleeve.

"Told you I could come in handy," she boasts with a wink, stepping closer to me. "You okay?"

"Where the hell did you learn to do that?"

"You probably don't want to know, Detective Alvarez," she jokes, wrapping her arm around my waist to give my back a brief caress.

Chapter 8

Isabella

My hands won't stop shaking. I grip the steering wheel until my knuckles turn white as I drive back to the station. Adrenaline still courses through me. Today, we both could have died.

I steal glances at Crow. She's slipped back into her usual swagger, almost as if defusing a bomb was just the adrenaline kick her system craves. Or maybe, saving Marla Trenton, her first love, did the trick.

Facing death isn't new to me; since moving to Homicide, I've been in my share of shootouts. But today was different. The way Crow threw us to the ground, how she clung to me to shield me. Damn, I can still feel her warmth on my back.

I shake my head, trying to shake off those thoughts. She saved my life, and I'm grateful. That's all. It can't be more.

"You okay?" she whispers, her smile so warm it could melt the Arctic.

"Yeah," I snap back, a little too harsh.

"Hey, the first time you nearly get blown up is always a doozy. It's okay to be rattled," she jokes, crinkling her nose in that teasing way she has.

I manage a smile. I won't show weakness. But she's right; this hit me harder than I'd like to admit. It's not just the brush with death. She saved my life, and owing her, especially something this big, sits heavy with me. I don't know where the investigation will lead, but I might have to lock her up again. And I hate to admit it, but in those moments on the ground, her body against mine, our hearts beating together... damn, I felt an attraction I can't deny. Not to myself, anyway.

"You did good out there," she says, lightly brushing my hand on the gear shift.

Just a simple compliment, but it strikes deep. The thought of feeling something for this woman scares me more than any bomb.

Back at the station, Crow heads straight to the room where Marla Trenton waits. My colleagues have been questioning her, and as expected, she's clueless about why she was targeted. Through the one-way glass, I watch them embrace.

They chat easily, years of separation melting away with each passing second. Crow rests her hand on Marla's arm, punctuating her words with gentle touches. And when Marla reaches out to brush a strand of hair from Crow's face, I feel an unexpected twinge of jealousy.

Instinctively, I tense up, my fists clench. This makes no sense. Crow is just a means to an end. That's all. Unless she's involved and is a damn murderer.

Marla says something that makes Crow laugh, a comment I can't hear but still stings. For some reason, I wish I were the one to make her laugh like that, and it makes me nervous.

I find myself fixated on her neck as she throws her head back to laugh, the mischievous sparkle in those gorgeous blue eyes. Her lips slightly parted. Shit.

"Sorry to interrupt this little reunion," I growl, barging into the room. "We have a suspect to interrogate."

Crow looks at me, puzzled, as if to say the interrogation could surely wait another five minutes. I don't even know why I interrupted them like that.

"See you around, cutie," Marla says, winking at Crow in a way that churns my stomach.

I need to stop this.

***

"Let's go over this one more time," I threaten, slamming my hand on the table in the interrogation room as I lean in toward the suspect. "Who hired you?"

Jeremy Bennet squirms under the harsh light, a long list of run-ins with the law to his name, some still pending. This isn't his first rodeo, but discomfort etches across his face.

"I've told you a dozen times. Hired through the Dark Web. Never met the guy. Got half the payment upfront in Monero, the rest was promised on job completion. All anonymous."

"Man, the things I missed being in jail," Crow murmurs, seemingly intrigued by Monero's ring signatures that allow transactions without revealing any info.

"You must have a name, some way to contact this person. Give me something, Jeremy!" I press, raising my voice.

"All I know is he goes by Viper on the Dark Web. We only communicated electronically."

"And what exactly did Viper hire you to do?"

"Place the bomb in the apartment. Swear I didn't even know who it was for. Kidnapping that woman in broad daylight? Alone? Ridiculous. How was I supposed to do that? My only job was to plant the bomb, following Viper's instructions," Bennet confesses, his nervousness peaking as he realizes the gravity of attempted murder charges.

My gut screams he's just a pawn. Not the mastermind, but we need more.

Catching Crow's signal from the corner of my eye, I grunt, "This better be good," and follow her out.

"This isn't working," she snaps once we're alone.

"Oh, because you're the interrogation expert?"

"You'd be surprised at the interrogations I've seen. Trust me, you wouldn't want to replicate those here. Too messy with blood," she jests.

"Can you track down this Viper on the Dark Web?"

"That's naive. He'll just change his alias anytime he wants a job done."

"So, what's your brilliant theory? You look eager to show off how smart you are," I grumble, unable to hide my annoyance.

"That guy's telling the truth. Marla was just bait to get us rushing to the apartment. The bomb wasn't meant for her."

"For you then?"

"Nope."

"For... was it meant for me?" I ask, the fear evident in my voice.

"Yep."

"What the hell makes you think that?"

"They knew I'd spot the bomb placement. It wasn't meant for me," she states, leaving it at that.

Once again, she leaves me feeling like she's three steps ahead. That aftertaste of knowing something she's not ready to share. Crow's like those damn black roses she used in each of her crimes. Beauty mingled with darkness. A criminal with a weird ethical code in her deeds. Right and wrong.

"Got any ideas, or just want to rub in that I'm getting nowhere?" I snap.

"Charge him with the two murders."

"Fuck, Crow. I can't do that."

"But he doesn't know that," she shrugs. "He's used to dealing with cops over petty stuff. The threat of two murders plus an attempt on a law enforcement officer? He'll wet his pants."

I shake my head. Crow's idea is logical but lacks ethics.

"Shelly, found anything?" I ask, dialing up cybercrimes.

She tells me they've set up surveillance software in case Viper shows up on the Dark Web looking to hire again, but nothing's come up yet.

"He won't get caught that way," Crow adds, rolling her eyes in disdain. "I know how people like him think. He's not dumb enough to use the same alias. But having that tracker doesn't hurt. You never know."

"Do you think he'd use the same forum to hire another hitman? Even under a different name?"

"It wouldn't surprise me. For all we know, he doesn't even realize we've nabbed Bennett. Your best move is to scare him. Really scare him," she emphasizes.

With a deep sigh, I march back into the interrogation room, Crow in tow, ready to play my last card, fully aware of its questionable legality.

"Here's the deal, Bennett. For now, I'm pinning two related murders on you, plus today's attempted homicide... unless you give me something concrete on this Viper character. And I mean now!" I threaten, raising my voice.

Just as Crow predicted, Jeremy's face goes white.

"I haven't killed anyone," he breathes out, burying his face in his hands.

"You're our prime suspect," I state, shrugging nonchalantly.

Sweat begins to bead on his forehead. He's terrified.

Chapter 9

Isabella

"I'm still waiting, Bennett," I growl, standing over him, leaning forward with my hands pressed flat on the table. "Give me something on Viper, or I'll slap you with two murders and today's attempted homicide. Time's ticking, tick tock, tick tock. And my patience is running thin."

Jeremy Bennett looks up at me, his forehead now drenched in sweat.

"Come on, Jeremy, don't be an idiot. Give me something, a name, a location, anything. This is your best shot at avoiding a life sentence," I press.

I can see him starting to crack. He shifts uneasily in the metal chair, his eyes darting around, looking for an escape. He slumps, crushed under the weight of the new accusations. It's a scene I've witnessed too many times. He's on the brink of breaking.

Bennett lets out a long sigh, still torn between facing a possible life sentence or the wrath of the man who hired him. He bites the inside of his cheek, his jaw muscles tensing.

It's almost there.

"Alright, Bennett, have it your way," I insist, pretending to leave the room.

"Wait!" he yells. "There was a plan B. Only if I couldn't place the bomb at the apartment," he admits, covering his face with his hands.

"I'm listening," I say softly, sitting down across from him.

"The Yacht Club on River Street. It's some fundraiser gala, I don't know exactly what for. It's going to be crowded. Marla Trenton will be there. If the bomb plan fell through, my job was to swing by the club and wait for her. Just to scare her, I swear," he rushes to explain. "Scare her good, Viper gave me carte blanche."

"What do you mean he gave you freedom?" Crow interjects, stepping dangerously close to Bennett.

"I swear I wasn't going to hurt her, but Viper told me I could do whatever I wanted with her," Bennett says, raising his hands and avoiding Crow's gaze.

"Is that all you've got for me?" I ask sharply, looking to press him further.

"That's all I've got, I swear. Please, tell me this will count for something. I've told you everything I know," he adds, his voice laced with nerves.

Without a word, I stand and exit the interrogation room, Crow following closely. She tosses one last threatening glance at Bennett.

"Are you on a diet of air or something?" she quips, nodding at the clock on the wall.

"Are you upset about something?"

"I'm starving. In movies, cops are always munching on donuts, and you haven't offered me a single one, detective," she teases, her eyebrows raised.

"How does a burger sound? My treat. I owe you one."

Crow nods, and soon, we're enveloped in the scent of greasy burgers from the diner across from the station. We slide into the worn red vinyl seats, Crow sporting a grin that stretches from ear to ear.

"You like this place?"

"I like that you don't — live a little, detective. Not everything in life is about staying fit."

Before I know it, Crow orders an absurd amount of food for both of us. It seems her only criterion was the grease content, not actual preference, but somehow, her laid-back vibe eases me too.

Soon, a mountain of nachos smothered in melted cheese lands in front of us, which Crow eyes as if she hasn't eaten in a month.

"Wow, this is amazing," she confesses, eyes closed in appreciation.

I shrug and nibble on a few. Not a huge fan of cheese-laden nachos, but the burger's pretty good.

"Try this sauce," Crow says, dipping a nacho in spicy tomato sauce and extending it towards my mouth.

I don't know if it's the spice of the nacho or the act of Crow feeding it to me, but I start sweating more than I'd like.

Our fingers accidentally touch over a plate of fries next to the nachos. I pull away, mumbling a quick apology, but my heart skips several beats. The next time, Crow leaves her hand lingering a bit longer, seeking contact I'm desperately trying to avoid.

Conversation flows comfortably, and for the first time, I'm truly enjoying myself alone with her. She seems in a good mood, each of her smiles breaking through like sunlight through clouds. But her lips, so captivating, stir something in the pit of my stomach at the thought of kissing them, impossible to ignore.

"You've got a bit of sauce there, don't move," she whispers suddenly.

Frozen, I couldn't move even if I wanted to. Crow traces my lower lip with her fingertip so delicately that my entire body trembles.

She smiles, fully aware of the effect she's having. Leaning in slowly. So slowly, it feels like time has stopped. I'm lost in the depths of those piercing blue eyes staring into mine, a sultry feline gaze that's melting me.

Damn. My pulse pounds in my temples. I should get up, make some excuse about the bathroom, anything, but the desire in her eyes is making me lose my head, and she knows it.

Part of me fights to resist. I hold my breath as she moves closer, inch by tantalizing inch, those beautiful lips parted. The world shrinks down to just the two of us.

Another smile, this one playful and sweet. She has me, and I'm an idiot for letting it happen.

"Detective," she breathes, her mouth so close I can feel the heat. Unable to stop myself, my lips part slightly.

Crow tilts her head, eyes dropping to my mouth. I mirror her movements instinctively, not daring to breathe, lids growing heavy, and then...

"Fuck!" Crow huffs, pulling back and rolling her eyes skyward.

My phone rings, shattering the moment. I let out an involuntary sigh of relief. Saved by Chief Davis.

"Yes sir, you got it," I tell him, hanging up.

"What's up?" Crow asks, clearly annoyed at the interruption.

"We need to check out that yacht club gala. Chief Davis scored tickets, thinks we might spot something since Marla was attending."

"Going as a couple then?" She raises a brow.

"Going together. Undercover."

"Well, you know, we should pretend a little, right? Might look weird if you're ten feet away the whole time. You kinda scream 'cop' from a mile off," Crow teases, making quote fingers.

"You have anything fancy to wear?"

"Not really big on dances in the joint."

"Chief said we can pop into a shop and get you a dress. There's a nice boutique a few blocks over." I lay a fifty on the table as I stand.

"Buying me a dress? That's so romantic, Izzy!" She nudges me playfully.

"This is serious business, and don't call me that."

"You're no fun," she murmurs, smiling.

At the store, Crow seems to enjoy trying on outfit after outfit before holding up an elegant black strapless number. "What do you think?"

"Whatever you want is fine."

"I should get matching underwear. These sports bras won't work. No bra at all might look better. What do you think, sexy black lingerie set or just go commando?"

I start to protest, but she reads my expression and laughs. "Kidding! I'll try this on." She winks, pretending to fiddle with a bra as she heads to the dressing room.

Alone with my thoughts, I shouldn't be picturing Crow undressing, or imagining how that lingerie might hug her curves, or how her back would arch under my touch if we made love.

Chapter 10

Isabella

At an event that's supposedly about raising funds, the sheer extravagance of the gala itself screams money burning. A live jazz band serenades the cream of New York's high society, who are too busy sipping their drinks and making deals to really care about the cause. I guess, for them, being seen is more important than what they're actually here for.

I take my time scanning the glitzy ballroom, every sense on high alert for any hint of danger. Crow's right there with me, stunning in her black dress but obviously out of her element among all this luxury and the fake smiles that don't quite reach people's eyes.

"Could you maybe not cling to my waist and focus?" I grumble.

"We're supposed to be a couple, detective," she whispers back, a playful twinkle in her eye as she casually rests a hand on my hip.

"See anything out of place?" I press on.

"Besides that ridiculous mermaid ice sculpture?"

"What about that guy by the bar?" I nod subtly in his direction.

"The one nursing a whiskey?"

"Yeah, him."

"He definitely looks like he could be our guy. More thug than tycoon. There's this uneasy vibe about him, like he's pissed about something. Maybe he was expecting someone who's a no-show," she muses, squinting his way.

"Crow, do you need glasses?"

"What the hell are you talking about?"

"Crow... I can't believe this. Tell me, what does the sign right next to him say?" I ask, trying to confirm my suspicions.

"You questioning my literacy now? I told you, I read a lot in jail."

"Scared of covering those pretty blue eyes with glasses?" I tease.

"I didn't think one Martini would get you this loopy, detective," she retorts with a grimace, but doesn't deny her poor eyesight.

"We need to get closer. He fits the bill perfectly. Big, buff, bald. That tux is screaming for mercy. If he so much as flexes, it's gonna rip. We just need a peek at that tattoo to confirm, but I can't see it from here unless he turns around. He has to be our guy. The one the jeweler described."

I watch him more intently. The guy scans the room with controlled aggression, like he's on the lookout for someone specific or expecting something to happen at any moment.

"He's on high alert. The moment he sees someone making a beeline for him, he'll bolt," Crow assures me.

"Not if we waltz up to him," I suggest, with what I hope is a stroke of genius.

"Wow, detective. If a single Martini has you inviting me to dance, I can't imagine what two or three would do," she teases, biting her lower lip and raising her eyebrows in mock anticipation.

Choosing not to bite, I simply extend my hand towards her, praying she doesn't notice the blush I feel creeping up my neck.

"You sure know how to treat a lady," she laughs, taking my hand and leading us onto the dance floor.

I roll my eyes, silently. Crow enjoys pushing my buttons, and there are moments I can't decide whether to slap her or pin her against a wall and kiss her senseless.

Or, you know, other things I'm trying not to think about right now because the moment we step onto the dance floor, the rest of the world just fades away. I place my hands on her waist, a little shyly at first, but Crow dives into her role, draping her arms around my neck and pulling me close, resting her head on my shoulder.

As we sway slowly to the music, the warmth of her body, the scent of her perfume, the brush of her breasts against mine, and her fingertips gently caressing the back of my neck are overwhelming. I'm supposed to focus on the mission, but my quickened heartbeat and short breaths tell a different story.

"We're close. Can you see the tattoo?" Crow whispers near my ear, feigning a move to kiss behind my earlobe.

I doubt the soft sigh that escapes me counts as an answer, and I hope Crow's gentle purring as she nuzzles my neck is just her way of teasing.

"Yeah, it's him," I admit, my knees practically shaking.

"Let's get a closer look," she suggests.

Suddenly, Crow tenses, her gaze darting nervously over my shoulder.

"Fuck!" she exclaims, right before cupping my face in her hands and pulling me into a kiss.

My mind goes blank. I part my lips slightly, feeling the tip of her tongue trace them slowly, seeking mine, and the embarrassed moan I stifle against her mouth is the last thing I expected to hear.

Just as quickly, she breaks the kiss, leaving me dazed.

"Sorry, detective, I think he saw us. It was the best way to blend in," she confesses.

"Yeah, you're right," I agree, my pulse racing, barely able to think straight. "Damn, he's on the move."

The bald guy makes a beeline for the exit. From the back, the snake tattoo on his neck is unmistakably clear.

Sneakily, I dash after him. He shoves past guests, his massive frame looking even more out of place as he flees.

"Police, stop!" I yell, seeing him start to slip away, but he doesn't halt.

Hitting the cold night air, the chill slaps me awake. He's surprisingly fast for his size. Still, ditching my heels, I close the gap.

Feeling me close in, the guy spins around lightning-fast and swings at me with his massive fist, aiming right at my left cheek. I try dodging, positioning my body to take the hit less squarely, but it doesn't stop me from crashing to the ground, dazed for a few moments.

"Thank goodness you box," Crow teases, squatting down beside me.

"He got away," I curse, vision still blurry.

"Hey, now we know he's right-handed. Or ambidextrous," she adds with a wink. "Let's get inside and put some ice on that."

Leaning on her shoulder, we hobble back towards the yacht club when I notice Crow's fist clenched around something shiny.

"Seriously, Crow?" I huff, annoyed. "Please tell me you weren't stealing in there."

"Hey, come on. What do you take me for? A criminal?" She feigns innocence. "It fell from baldy with the snake tattoo while he was running. Do you know how much this is worth?" she asks, waving the glittering watch in the air.

Chapter 11

Isabella

"Hand it over, Crow!" I demand.

"First, let's get some ice on that bruise. I'll keep it safe in the meantime."

"Crow, give me the watch. It's evidence," I insist, reaching out my hand.

"I don't know what you take me for. I was just holding onto it temporarily, you know, since you're a bit woozy from that punch. Not like I was planning to keep it or anything," she grumbles, placing it in my palm.

"Is it expensive?"

"A Patek Philippe Calatrava in white gold? Super expensive," Crow replies without hesitation. "No clue how that guy could afford it. But hey, maybe this will lead you to a jeweler who keeps reliable records of what they sell," she adds.

I secure the watch in my bag, and as we head back to the yacht club, I can't help but think maybe I was too quick to doubt Crow. She could have taken the time to stash that watch away. Instead, she kept it in her fist to get back to me faster. I guess it's hard not to remember her past. Can someone like her change? Is it possible for a criminal with a long rap sheet to reform?

"I'm sorry, it's not that I doubt you," I rush to clarify. "Any idea how he might have gotten it?"

"Probably swiped it from one of those club snobs who hasn't even noticed it's missing. Wealth redistribution, I guess," she jokes, requesting a bag of ice from the bar.

The fancy gala seems to dissolve into the fog as she applies ice to my cheek, her brow furrowed, like she's worried about something.

"Are you sure you're okay?" she presses. "You'd look quite sexy with a little scar on your cheek," she teases, tapping the tip of my nose lightly, leaving me speechless.

Just when I'm about to reply, my worst nightmare unfolds.

"Isabella Alvarez... quite the spectacle for the NYPD: dancing and kissing a known criminal you're supposed to be investigating," I hear from behind me.

I don't need to turn around to know who's spewing those words.

"I'm not investigating her... Crow, I'm not investigating you," I assure her, my voice dropping with those last words.

I don't know why I feel the urge to explain myself instead of standing up and shutting her up.

"What are you doing here, Kalinsky?" I snap, my tone dripping with disdain.

"I'm here with my partner," she boasts, approaching a man who's at least thirty years her senior but reeks of money. "And you two? On a romantic getaway?"

"We're on an investigation. Orders from Chief Davis."

"Oh, I'm sure Chief Davis explicitly ordered you to make out with the criminal on the dance floor. He'll be thrilled to hear you've followed his orders to the letter," she sneers, shooting a challenging look at Crow. "You've always been obsessed with that criminal," she adds, her face twisting in disgust.

"Enough, Kalinsky!" I raise my voice, my frustration boiling over. "We hit the dance floor to close in on a suspect, and that kiss? It was all for show, a cover when we got near him. And since you're so keen on observations, maybe you can explain to Chief Davis why you didn't step in when the suspect bolted."

Luckily, her partner whispers something to her, noticing the scene we're causing, and she stops. Her face cycles through shades of red before she finds her voice again, eyes blazing with animosity.

"This isn't over, Alvarez," Kalinsky threatens before being whisked away by her companion.

I let out a huff, watching them disappear into the crowd, my anger vibrating through me until Crow's hand finds mine, her thumb soothingly stroking my knuckles.

69

"You know, my life was way simpler when Kalinsky was on my case. Clueless, that one. I half expected her to be kicked off the force by now," she quips with a smirk.

"She's a fool," I mutter under my breath.

"Let's get out of here, detective," she whispers, nodding towards the exit.

***

"I could've made it to my doorstep on my own, Crow," I grumble, squinting my eyes at her in the dim light of the New York streets.

"I just wanted to make sure you were okay after that hit, you know," she replies, shifting her weight from one leg to the other, a sure sign of nerves in her otherwise cool demeanor.

"Got something on your mind?" I ask, catching the flicker of hesitation in her eyes.

"It's just... I'm sorry for the trouble the kiss caused. Explaining that to Chief Davis won't be easy," she admits.

"Kalinsky's always been a piece of work. Don't sweat it," I assure her with a wave of my hand.

"Yeah, well, I... I shouldn't have kissed you without asking first and..."

"Crow," I sigh, and before I even know what I'm doing, I reach out, placing my hand on her waist and pulling her close, my lips finding

70

hers in a brief, soft kiss. It's quick, a mere brush really, but it sends my heart racing like it's trying to win a marathon.

"Wow, guess that makes us even," she jokes, but the spark in her eyes tells me she's far from satisfied. Craves more. A lot more.

"Did that bother you?" I ask, my voice tinged with a hint of worry.

"Are you kidding me?" she laughs, her voice low and husky. "Feel free to do that again, anywhere on me you like," Crow adds, her wink loaded with mischief.

"You wanna come up?" I whisper, suddenly aware that I might be on the brink of the biggest blunder of my life, but completely unable to stop myself.

"Sure, but just to make sure you don't get dizzy on your way to your apartment. No fantasies, detective," she teases.

"For the record, I've wanted to give you that kiss for a long time," I confess as I fumble with the keys to my place.

The only reply I get is the pressure of Crow's body against mine, pinning me to the wall as she kicks the front door closed. My heart hammers against my ribcage when I feel her warmth enveloping me. She tugs at my hair, gently forcing my neck to the side, her lips crashing against mine with a passion that sets every nerve alight.

Her tongue traces my lower lip, and before I can catch my breath, she hikes up my dress, her right hand slipping beneath my underwear, fingers dancing between my legs.

71

"Are you in a rush?" I gasp out.

"You have no idea," she whispers right into my ear, before her hands grip the sides of my panties, tearing them with a boldness that sends shivers down my spine.

In a fleeting moment of clarity, I catch myself realizing the sheer foolishness of what I'm doing. Sure, excitement courses through me — intense, undeniable excitement — but it's tangled up with confusion and fear. Trust in her isn't my strong suit, and if word of this gets out, I'm toast. If Crow's mixed up in these crimes, my little escapade could blow everything sky-high.

But that flash of clarity? It's just that — a flicker. It's drowned out by my own moans as I feel her fingers inside me, fogging up my ability to think straight.

"Just go with it," Crow breathes out, a smirk in her voice. I prop my right leg on a chair for better access, and her warmth presses closer.

I cling to her neck, feeling the heat radiating from her body, the passion in the way she strokes me, firm and precise. Every fear, every doubt, it all evaporates. There's only Crow.

My legs shake, her name escaping in ragged breaths. I'm pressed against the wall, unraveling into moans each time her fingers curl and coax a wild pleasure from deep within.

"Oh shit!" I shout, and my whole body trembles as an orgasm builds up inside me.

I grip Crow tighter, fingers threading through her hair, moaning, sighing her name while she whispers into my ear what she plans to do next. It's raw, it's intense, it's primal — but it's better than anything I've ever experienced.

Our hips move in sync, her fingers knowing exactly where to press to drive me wild. She kisses my neck, nips at my earlobe, and as I reach a breathtaking climax, one word slips from my throat in a broken whisper, "Crow."

Chapter 12

Isabella

"That was fucking amazing," Crow whispers, her fingers still lingering inside me as beads of sweat trace down my back.

I just nod slowly, fighting to catch my breath. She locks eyes with me, a hint of a smile on her lips.

"Where's the bedroom?" she breathes out, running her hand through my hair.

Wordlessly, we head to my room, clothes discarded like breadcrumbs behind us.

"I'm into those slight abs of yours, detective," she admits, her fingertips dancing across my stomach.

"I didn't figure you for being so in shape," I say, genuinely surprised.

"It's all that parkour."

"You do parkour?"

"Only when the cops are on my tail," Crow jokes, lying down next to me to plant a kiss.

I can't help but smile. There's just something about her that's getting under my skin.

I flip her onto her back, tracing one of her tattoos with my finger before my hand wanders to her breasts. She closes her eyes and lets out a sigh, a slight arch forming in her back as her nipples harden under my touch. And though I've imagined this moment, reality is knocking it out of the park.

Her body is a live wire, each touch, each kiss sends her shaking. And those nipples, caught by my mouth... fuck, they feel like the height of sensuality.

I follow the lines of a new tattoo with my lips, drifting down to her belly, and then lower. As I near her sex, Crow stretches out like a cat, soft moans slipping out, driving me wild with desire.

I pause to take her in. I blow gently across her clit, her back arching at the sensation. She writhes, anticipation crackling in the air. Her toes curl; Crow strokes my hair tenderly but stays silent. It's like she's savoring the sweet agony.

I kiss her sex, tasting her arousal, and soon her moans grow louder. She threads her hands through my hair, pulling me closer in a raw, urgent gesture as her hips rise to meet the rhythm of my tongue.

Before I know it, I'm devouring her as if we're on borrowed time. Crow gets lost in a symphony of moans and gasps, her right hand leaving my hair to tease her nipples until she lets out a long, soft moan and goes still, except for the little shivers of pleasure that quake through her hips.

"Wow, detective," she breathes out, head thrown back, eyes half-closed.

"I guess you can call me Izzy."

"I'm kinda liking 'detective'," she quips, pulling at my arms to drape my body over hers.

Crow's heart thumps against her chest, a rhythm I feel as she catches her breath. Gentle scratches trail down my back, descending to my butt for a playful spank before she seals it with a fervent kiss.

"I want to handcuff you to the bed," Crow blurts out suddenly.

"I'm not sure that's a good idea," I argue.

"Don't be a bore. Remember, you've cuffed me plenty of times. This will be way better," she assures me with a sly wink.

My heart skips a beat or two. Handcuffed to the bed, and with the official steel no less, courtesy of Crow? Yet, there's this undeniable thrill that's bubbling up inside me.

I'm practically quivering as she secures my wrists. A surge of adrenaline zips through me, electrifying. It's odd, being at her mercy, cuffed to the bed, open to whatever she desires. And it's more exhilarating than I ever imagined.

She explores my body with a touch that teases and tempts me. Fingertips glide over my skin, leaving goosebumps in their wake. Circling

76

my breasts, skirting the areola yet never touching the nipples, she has me begging.

She smiles.

"You're torturing me, Crow," I gasp, my breath hitching.

Leaning down, her tongue traces my neck, following the line of my jugular to my ear.

"I'm going to fuck you until you scream my name," she whispers, nipping at my earlobe.

And I have to admit, Crow delivers on that promise. My body twists under her hands. She caresses me with a tenderness that's maddening, kissing every inch of my skin so slowly. By the time she reaches my sex, I'm so wound up that it doesn't take much for me to come undone in a powerful climax.

Still trying to catch my breath, Crow releases the cuffs and pulls me into an embrace.

"Next time, we'll use something softer," she promises, rubbing the pink marks the metal left on my wrist.

She snuggles against me, head resting on my shoulder, arm curled around my waist, and the silence that fills the bedroom wraps around us like a cozy blanket.

I can't help but smile like a fool as she plants soft kisses along my collarbone. I kiss the top of her head, tuck a stray lock of hair behind her ear, and when she stretches to pull the blanket over us before we drift off to sleep, I find myself whispering an "I love you" into the quiet of the night.

***

The morning light sneaks through the curtains, and for a second, the warm skin of Crow pressed against mine has me smiling. She's curled up close, breathing easy, her arm draped right below my left tit.

Then reality hits me like a freight train. My heart kicks into overdrive. What the hell did I do?

"Fuck, I'm an idiot!" I mutter under my breath.

Carefully, I lift Crow's arm off me, trying not to wake her, and pad naked to the kitchen. Guilt squeezes my stomach. I've crossed a forbidden line. A whole bunch of them. If this gets out... if we end up in court because she's involved somehow... Shit, my career as a cop is toast.

I'm an idiot. Can't deny my feelings for her, but this is impossible. Last night was a moment of weakness I can't afford.

I grip the countertop so hard my knuckles turn white, and let out a choked scream of pure frustration.

Then, this weird feeling hits me. I can't shake it, and I bolt to the living room. Shit!

"Crow! Where's the watch?" I yell, rifling through her purse to find nothing but emptiness.

She ambles over, naked and bleary-eyed, rubbing her eyes.

"Waking up to that naked body, I'm pretty sure brings good luck," she jokes with a yawn.

"Where's the fucking watch?" I snap, slapping the table.

Her face drops, the smile gone. It's not anger, guilt, or regret. It's disappointment.

"You stuffed it in that drawer over there last night," she reminds me softly, her finger pointing to the living room's main piece. "You dropped it pulling out your phone, and decided to keep it safe."

"Shit, Crow, I'm sorry... I didn't..."

"It's okay. No big deal, I'm leaving."

"No, wait, Crow!" I say, guilt twirling my insides into knots.

"See you at the station tomorrow, detective. I know when I'm not wanted," she says before swiftly picking up her clothes and getting dressed in a rush.

"Crow..."

"Don't sweat it, Detective Alvarez. No one will hear about this from me," she says without even a glance back, heading out the door.

Chapter 13

Crow

The fluorescent lights at the police station are crueler today, glaring down as we wait on forensics to spill the secrets of that damn watch. Isabella hasn't really looked at me, as if last night was the biggest blunder of her life. For a few hours, I let myself imagine a future with her, hope curled up next to her bare skin like a cat in the sun.

But her lack of trust stabs me cold. That icy stare cuts deep, and I get it: I'm just a crook to her, trash to be tossed.

Her office air hangs thick. "Good morning" is all we've exchanged. Out of the corner of my eye, I catch her stealing glances. A couple of times, she almost speaks, but the words are cowardly, always retreating back down her throat. Whatever I thought we had with Isabella evaporated like morning mist.

And it stings. I'm no stranger to pain. My life's a highlight reel of the stuff, but this? This is brutal. I let my guard down for her, showed her the real me, and got served a plate of cold indifference. She can't see past my scars, fixated on the thorns and missing the rose entirely.

"If something's bugging you, just spit it out already," I blurt, the words hot and heavy with frustration.

"What?"

"Look, detective," I say, "I get that we don't have to be best friends or, heaven forbid, anything more. We're just working a case together, but don't treat me like I'm invisible."

Isabella just snorts, rolls her eyes, and doesn't even bother with a comeback. She's flipped the switch to 'hard-ass detective' mode, and I'm back to being the con she had to slap cuffs on eight years ago.

"Any updates?" Isabella's voice snaps like a whip as one of the forensics team steps in.

She's out of her chair like it's on fire, like sharing space with me is the last place on earth she wants to be.

"High-ticket items like that are usually well-documented," the investigator pipes up, a hint of pride in his voice. "We touched base with the jewelry store that sold it. Looks like the owner is one Héctor Rummage."

"The financier?" I cut in, my voice dripping with a mix of surprise and skepticism.

Isabella nods, her eyes narrowing like she's adding up figures in her head. "He's got her fingers in a lot of pies—everything from tech startups to, uh, diverse holdings."

"Yeah, including those vulture funds that snap up buildings in low-income areas and squeeze the life out of tenants. And when they're not harassing them to leave, they're bulldozing their homes to pop up shopping malls. And they call me a criminal," I scoff, rolling my eyes to the heavens.

"Rummage has been under the microscope a few times for, let's say, 'questionable activities'," the forensics guy chimes in, shooting a quick, wary glance at Isabella, like he's worried he's stepped in it by spilling the beans in front of me.

"And why did the thug at the charity gala have his watch?" I ask, my curiosity piqued.

"Has she reported it stolen?" Isabella tosses the question into the ring, her voice cool and even.

"Hey, I think my question already had yours tucked inside it," I protest, my words tinged with a playful bite.

Isabella doesn't take the bait, just squints her eyes and shakes her head, a small but determined refusal. She takes a deep breath, before snagging her jacket from the coat rack.

"We're rolling out," she declares. "Let's drop in on Rummage. Maybe we'll shake something loose."

Isabella

It hurts to ice Crow out, but I tell myself it's for the best—for both of us. Last night's slip-up can't happen again. It's just off-limits from every angle you look at it.

I get it; she's like a hit of something too good, dangerously addictive. There's this pull she has, and I can't seem to fight it. So, I think the best defense is a good offense. Keep our worlds from colliding too much.

The financial district is a whole other beast, with parking spots as rare as a chill day for me. So, we ditch the car in a lot and hoof it, cutting through an alley that's seen better days.

Stepping in, my senses go on high alert. I hate places like this. I take a few deep breaths, like Karen, my therapist for years, taught me. Our footsteps echo off the concrete, and with every step, my heartbeat goes a little more rogue.

I can't help scoping out every possible hidey-hole for threats. All I see are dumpsters, spilling over with black bags, belching out that sickening stench of rot, mixed with the sharp tang of urine from a wall.

Then, this rat, the size of a small cat, darts from a cardboard fortress, and I freeze. An old, sharp memory jabs at me, taking the wheel.

I'm back to being twenty-three-year-old Isabella Álvarez, green and gutsy, fresh out of the academy. I was patrolling with my partner in an alley just like this one. We were checking out a domestic disturbance call—supposed to be routine. Things were fine until the guy got twitchy and pulled a gun. Pete, he was all about keeping it cool, trying to talk the guy down, but I freaked, my hand instinctively going for my gun...

Time slows to a crawl. Two shots ring out. I'm frozen, paralyzed by the sound. Hunkered down on the ground, my eyes slam shut. Pete's body hits the pavement next to me, lifeless.

Fear roots me to the spot. His blood spreads out in a vast crimson pool, staining the concrete. His eyes stare at me, wide with disbelief, as if, even in death, they're questioning why I didn't shield him.

I remember screaming, a muffled, soul-tearing sound. Screaming until my throat feels raw. I clutched his lifeless body, begged him to hang on. Through sobs, I pleaded with the arriving EMTs to save him, but it was already too late.

He was six months from retirement.

Even now, the memory haunts me. I wake up gripping Pete's body, screaming into the void. The guilt and horror of that night have left a scar no amount of therapy can heal.

"Jesus, you okay, detective?" Crow's voice snaps me back. My eyes flutter open. She's looking at me, brow knitted with concern, probably wondering if I've lost it.

Suddenly, tires screech against the pavement. The noise grabs my attention. Everything happens too fast to process. The sound of gunfire, deafening. Storefront windows shatter, raining glass down on us. Crow shoves me to the ground, shielding me with her body.

I'm barely aware of what's happening. I cover my face with my hands, ducking my head, and when I look again, my palms are smeared with blood.

"Crow," I gasp.

Chapter 14

Crow

"Ouch, detective, that's one heck of a gash on your forehead. You okay?" I ask, eyeing the glass shard that's too close to her eyebrow, trickling blood like a tiny crimson river.

"What the hell was that?"

"Gunfire, maybe?"

"I can see that, Crow. But, seriously, do you think it was random, or are they gunning for us?" Isabella insists, her voice tense.

"Random? No, people don't just stroll around the city shooting for fun. Someone's got an argument with you, sweetheart," I shrug.

"With me?"

"Or they're trying to scare you real good. Hold still so I can get that glass out."

Isabella looks at her hands, smeared with blood, her face a mask of shock and disbelief.

"Got it, let me clean that up," I whisper, pulling out a handkerchief from my pocket and pressing it against the wound. "I promise it's snot-free," I quip, trying to coax some color back into her pale cheeks.

"Is it deep?"

"It'll leave a scar. You wanna see a doc for some stitches?"

She shakes her head slowly, her gaze drifting to the end of the alley where the shots had come from. I grab her hand, and we sit down on some plastic crates against the wall that look a bit cleaner than the rest.

"Crow... thanks again. I..."

"I'm your partner, right? At least for this case. Partners cover each other, seen it in the movies. But hey, if you're offering another burger, I'm not saying no," I say with a wink.

Isabella goes silent for a moment. She lets out a long breath, tilting her head back while pressing down on her wound.

"I was cold to you this morning, I..."

"You were an ass, but I get it, it's cool," I cut her off.

"You know that thing after the charity gala should never have happened, right?" she asks, locking eyes with me.

"We've got a job to do, detective. Chasing down that bastard is what matters," I rush to say, forcing a smile, even though it feels like I'm breaking inside.

When she steadies herself and stands up, I don't waste time sharing my hunch.

"That shootout... it was too calculated. Either they've been tailing us from the start, or someone tipped them off about our visit to Hector Rummage," I say, clicking my tongue.

"There's no mole in my unit," she protests.

"Are you sure? Because those shooters seemed pretty clued in on our movements."

"They must have followed us from the start," Isabella says, handing me back my bloodied handkerchief, but I wave her off, gesturing to toss it in one of the nearby trash cans.

"Face it, you've got a rat in your department. That little fireworks show? Way too convenient for their liking. And your snail's pace didn't exactly help our cause," I quip, stretching my arms out in a mock surrender.

Isabella just huffs, a silent show of defiance, and smoothes out her blouse with the palms of her hands, trying to brush off leaves that clung like unwanted memories from our dive to the pavement. Another huff escapes her as she only manages to smear more blood across the fabric.

"I'd keep an eye on that smug-faced detective we bumped into at the yacht club," I mutter, giving her shoulder a nudge.

"Kalinsky might be a pain, but she's not behind this."

"Yeah, well, if there's one thing I've picked up in my line of work, it's that anyone can surprise you, given the right price or pressure," I add, rolling my eyes and shaking my head for emphasis.

"Enough, Crow," she protests, her voice inching up the scale.

"Alright, alright, have it your way. But someone's singing, unless you think those guys have psychic powers. I just want you safe and for you to know who you can trust," I add, my touch gentle on her arm.

"I trust you, Crow," she blurts out, stealing my breath away.

Those words tumble out before she can catch them, and we lock eyes, a half-smile playing on her lips. I choose to stay silent. Memories from that night swirl in my head, but I'm certain of one thing—I'd cover her through hell itself.

But our fleeting moment of connection shatters too soon. A message lights up her phone, draining the color from her face as she reads it.

"This investigation ends now. The next bullet won't miss," she growls under her breath.

"Let me guess. From someone in the know about our little adventure?"

"It seems so," Isabella admits.

"I hate to say I told you so, but... there it is. It's gotta be someone from your unit," I say, nodding slowly, feeling the weight of each word.

"Can you trace the number?"

"Doubt it's worth a shot, detective. Bet it's a burner tossed away already."

Isabella hesitates, her eyes darting around as she processes. Then, she lifts her gaze and nods.

"We've still got a date with Rummage," she reminds me, determination etched in her eyes.

"Looking like that? Your place is just two blocks away. Why don't we clean up that cut? Then, you can crash for a bit and hit up Hector Rummage later. I bet you've got a story to spill about the shootout," I add, nodding at two officers stepping out of their cruiser, approaching with that wary cop-walk, like they can't decide if we're victims or villains.

Once Isabella flashes her badge, and gives them the Cliff Notes version of our little street drama, promising to follow up with a report, I sidle up to her. I reach out, tilting her chin gently to get a good look at the wound. "Needs a good clean, at least. We don't want it getting nasty, and trust me, this alley's got more germs than a public restroom."

"It's nothing," she insists, with that stubborn tilt to her chin.

"You're as stubborn as they come, detective. Let's head to your place and fix you up, or to a doc. Your call,"

Isabella hesitates, chewing on the inside of her cheek, but then, sense wins over stubbornness, and she nods.

***

"Sorry, I know it stings," I murmur, noticing Isabella flinch a little when I dab antiseptic on her wound.

"It's part of the job," she grunts, all tough-as-nails detective.

"Yeah, lucky your buddies showed up just in time to save the day. What was it, half an hour later?"

Her eyes narrow, but there's a ghost of a smile on her lips.

"All done," I announce, letting my fingers linger just a second longer than necessary, tracing the line of her jaw with the faintest touch. "Now, you should get some rest."

"Thanks," she whispers, then, she grabs my jacket lapels and pulls me toward her.

Words aren't needed, not now.

Her arms loop around my neck, and her lips catch mine. First, it's soft, hesitant, like she's testing the waters—or maybe asking for permission. Then it's urgent, a silent plea spelled out in the press of her mouth against mine. She tangles her fingers in my hair as I straddle her lap. Her hand sneaks up my back, lifting my blouse, sneaking underneath to stroke my skin with a tenderness that belies her tough exterior.

The tip of her tongue traces my lips, seeking, inviting, and each kiss she lands sends a shiver down my spine. But then, a warning light flickers on in the back of my mind.

"I think... I think we should stop here. Sorry," I gasp out, stepping back.

Isabella throws her head back, a huff of frustration escaping her as her eyes close. She slumps against the couch, disappointment written all over her.

"Crow," she murmurs, tugging at my hand, trying to bring me back.

"We both know you'll regret it in the morning, and I'm not about to be your bad decision," I hiss, even as I lean down to steal one last kiss that leaves me wanting more.

Chapter 15

Isabella

I grip the phone with fury, the orders from Chief Davis boiling in my ear. "Stay home for a couple of days," he says, as if he's not aware someone's keeping us from getting too cozy with Hector Rummage. Trust is a luxury I can't afford now, and somebody's working overtime to keep it that way.

Slamming the phone down, I slump into the couch, exhaling a long, weary sigh. I don't wanna believe it, but maybe Crow's on to something. Could be a mole in my unit, and the thought's got me spiraling into full-blown paranoia.

Everything I've been trained to uphold's getting flipped on its head. Trust the system, your squad's got your six, follow orders without a blink.

Today's shootout ripped a hole in my trust. If one of our own leaked our location, who's left to trust? Even Chief Davis's 'resting' orders could be a smokescreen to buy Rummage time.

"So, what would you do?" I ask, the question hanging in the air like a thick fog.

Crow's eyes pop, her face a picture of disbelief.

"Think the worst, and you're probably right, detective. If I were you, I'd ghost the system during your little enforced break, keep digging. Worst case, you get a scolding from Davis. Best case, you nab the one pulling the strings. If there's a rat, trusting your buddies is a no-go until you sniff 'em out. A chewing out beats the alternative."

"And the alternative is?"

"Getting killed," she deadpans, like we're discussing the weather. "Look, things are getting dicey around here. Every step forward, we hit a new wall, and the stakes? Sky-high. I'd vanish," she says with a shrug, like it's the easiest thing in the world.

"Vanishing isn't exactly simple," I mutter.

Crow leans in, her voice a conspiratorial whisper, "You're wired, right? Got trackers?"

"I've got a personal tracker and a device on my phone. Both ping my location in real time. My car's got a GPS tracker that signals to the precinct, too. Necessary evils for our safety," I explain to her.

"Okay, leave the personal tracker here for a couple of days. It'll keep beeping your spot, and they'll think you're homebound. As for your phone, I can hook you up with a VPN to disguise your real locale, make 'em believe you're playing couch potato. Best move, with the way things are, would be to clone your phone. Leave the twin at home so it keeps pulling texts and calls," Crow suggests, her voice all business.

"And why's that?" I cut in.

"They're going to great lengths. Wouldn't be surprised if they try to sniff you out through the cell network. I can slap on some spyware, fake out your phone's IMEI. It's like giving your mobile a new set of fingerprints," she offers.

"That's my mobile's identity, right?"

"Bingo."

"Damn, what a rabbit hole we're down," I grumble, my hands cradling my face in frustration.

"The car's easy. Park it in the garage, end of story. I can borrow a bike if you need wheels."

"Borrow doesn't mean steal, does it?" I ask, raising an eyebrow, not fully trusting her brand of 'borrowing.'

"Man, you come up with the wildest stuff. I'll ask a friend," she says, rolling her eyes as if the idea of stealing something is foreign to her.

An hour later, according to the police department, I'm at home, resting. That's where I'll be for the next two days, while in reality, I'm closing my eyes tight as Crow guns a high-powered motorcycle way too fast en route to Hector Rummage's office.

"It's all gonna be fine, detective," Crow yells over the roar of the engine, and all I can do is hold on tighter to her waist with every sharp turn, our knees closer to the asphalt than I'd like.

In Rummage's office, I'm fighting to keep a lid on my anger. Usually, I'm patient in interrogations, but today's not my day. I'm itching to slam my hand on that fancy mahogany desk and demand some straight answers.

"Detective Alvarez, I'm no saint, that's clear. Still, I'm a businessman—a significant one—and I value my money. I'm not dumb enough to gift a white gold Patek Philippe Calatrava to a stranger," he says with a sneer.

For someone routinely mixed up with all sorts of shady dealings, he comes off as a pompous idiot. Lucky for him, he's got the cash to afford a slick team of lawyers who always manage to wiggle him out of trouble.

Lucky for him, too, I can't press too hard, because technically, I'm not even here. I can't risk him whining to my superiors, assuming he's not already cozy with someone at the station and he's not the one behind this mess.

Forty-five minutes later, and we're still spinning in circles – no useful info snagged. He denies everything, and the kicker? We've got zilch on him.

"Thanks for the chat. I've got a hunch we'll be seeing each other again," I say, clicking my tongue in annoyance.

Leaving empty-handed twists the initial fury into something gnarlier. It's been a real dumpster fire of a day, and I'm at a loss for the next moves.

"Mind if I take a crack at it?" Crow pipes up, catching me mid-punch at a wall.

"You thinking of playing cop?"

"Think about it, Isabella. Your gig and mine? Not worlds apart. Except, I've got way fewer rules to play by," she says, arching an eyebrow, "I can dabble in... let's just say, creativity with legality."

"God, Crow, you're driving me nuts! Spit it out already," I snap.

"Easy, detective," she winks, "Here's what I'd do: hack into Hector Rummage's system, poke around his financial statements, his emails. It's what the cops would do."

"Just minus the warrant."

"Details, details. By the time you get one, which – let's be real – won't happen because you can't pin anything on him, any dirt he's got will be long gone."

"And if – purely hypothetically – you did that, couldn't they trace it back to my place or yours?"

"Sure, your cybercrimes lady is sharp. Could probably catch me," she admits, "That's why we'd use a burner location. Got a buddy who owes me a favor or two. We could crash there while you're 'resting' at your place. But hey, I'm just theorizing here. You know I can't do any of that stuff – parole rules and all," she says, with a twinkle in her eye.

Chapter 16

Isabella

The safe house Crow's scrounged up, nestled in some industrial nook of the city, is stark, austere, almost monastic. Its bare walls sport nothing but the occasional crack. A sliver of light sneaks past the thick curtains, spotlighting dust particles dancing in the air like tiny, aimless ghosts.

I'm used to cop safe houses, but this one? It's like a layover for specters, a sort of limbo between worlds. It's not for living, just a brief haunt for a few days, a week tops. A hidey-hole to vanish from the law's prying eyes or dodge some rival gang's crosshairs. An empty shell of a place, identity scrubbed clean.

Crow didn't sweat breaking into her old criminal Rolodex to land it, and though it irks me that she's still got those shady speed dials, I can't knock its handiness right now.

Inside, my cop soul squirms, rattled in its cage. Lines were clear once – good guys, bad guys. Now? It's all smudged, and I'm adrift, anchorless.

"The software's chugging along. We'll be in soon," Crow announces, her hand landing on my shoulder, giving it a reassuring squeeze. Like she senses the storm of doubts in me.

"Please, just swear again they can't tie you to this hack job. I don't want you gambling with jail time," I press.

"No problem, detective," she says.

"And you're not gonna funnel off his funds if you crack into his accounts," I add, voice dipping low.

Crow locks me with those blue eyes, mischief twinkling. A wink is all the answers I get.

Her fingers tap out a rhythm on the keyboard, the only sound piercing the eerie quiet. Weirdly, I'm not as on edge as I should be. Here I am, letting Crow jack a known financier's network, while we're hunkered down in a crook's crash pad. But I guess desperate times call for desperate hacks, right? I'm just banking on Crow being as slick as she was back in her heyday.

"You know, this gig was a cakewalk before you slapped cuffs on me," she grumbles, lost in keystrokes, "Encryption's become a real beast."

"When did you start hacking, anyway?"

"I was sniffing around neighbors' Wi-Fi by, like, twelve," she admits with a wistful lilt, "Some kid showed me the ropes, and I just... ran with it. Never went to school much, so I had plenty of time to kill," she shrugs, casual as can be.

I bite back words, and she pauses, fingers still.

"You're probably crafting some tearjerker in your head," Crow says with a hint of sarcasm, "The tragic orphan girl who found solace in computers to escape her shitty life."

"I wasn't..." I start, but she cuts me off.

"Okay, yeah, you nailed it, that's exactly it," she admits, the corners of her mouth pulling into a strange smile. "That community center we visited... it saved me," she sighs, "They taught me to code there. The director said I had a gift. But it wasn't the programming that mattered most; it was being the first person who believed in me. The only one who showed me there was life beyond the streets. Her and Marla. Without that place, I'd probably end up on drugs, or worse."

I saw her connection with that center, "It gave you a purpose."

"It kept me out of most of the trouble in my neighborhood. That's why I funneled part of my earnings back to them. I can never repay what they did for me."

"That director... she seemed to think the world of you, too. She admired you," I confess.

"Easy with the praise, detective, you'll give a girl a big head," Crow jokes, her fingers dancing back to the keyboard.

"Can I ask you something?"

"Is it personal?"

"Kind of," I admit, biting my lower lip, "I want to understand some of your motivations better."

"In case you have to arrest me again?"

"Forget it, Crow," I sigh, letting out a puff of air.

"Shoot."

"Why the black roses? Was it just your signature, or did it mean something more?"

Crow raises an eyebrow, hesitating as if deciding whether to let me in on that secret.

"When I was a kid, my grandma had this tiny rose garden in our back patio. It was the one pretty thing in our crappy apartment. She loved tending to those flowers," she recalls, and I swear there's a hint of sadness there, her eyes glistening just a bit.

"Why black roses? Why not any other color?" I find myself asking, my curiosity getting the better of me.

Crow pauses, fingers fiddling with a frayed hole in her denim jeans. "My grandma used to say she saw beauty where others only saw the dark," she admits. "For me, black roses were like... elegance amidst chaos, you know? A reminder that what I was doing was more than just theft. Believe it or not, I had my own code of honor. I only hit those who got rich by stepping on others or through dirty deeds," she says, locking eyes with me, daring me to pass judgment.

We fall into silence again, but this time, it's different – comfortable, the kind where words just aren't necessary.

"What's on your mind?" she asks, swiveling her chair to grab my hand, giving it a reassuring squeeze.

"Oh, it's nothing. You'll think it's silly."

"Come on, spill. Or is it like, only you get to ask the deep stuff?"

I hesitate, then let it out. "I was thinking... maybe that rose is you. Beauty in the darkness."

She laughs softly, a light blush dusting her cheeks. "Keep saying things like that, and I won't be responsible for my actions, detective," she whispers.

Crow lets out a long breath, her eyes twinkling with mischief as she leans in closer. The tips of her fingers trail along my jaw, sending a shiver down my spine. I try to keep my cool, even as my heartbeat skips, when I notice her lips, slightly parted, inches from mine.

Then, the computer chimes – she's in. Crow's cracked Hector Rumange's network.

"Must be fate," she teases with a wink and a killer smile that could stop hearts.

Chapter 17

Isabella

"Okay, okay, what do we have here?" Crow hums, her knuckles lightly tapping against the computer's frame.

"What'd you find?" I lean in, the scent of her citrusy perfume weaving into my senses.

"The first thing you look for when big money's involved are offshore accounts," she explains, schooling me. "It's also the safest bet because, most of the time, these guys can't cry to the cops about it," she adds, arching an eyebrow.

"And I take it Hector Rummage has them?"

"The idiot named the file 'sunny holidays' like no one's gonna peek. Here, we've got accounts in Switzerland, Panama, and the Cayman Islands."

"Pity we can't use this in court," I mutter, frustrated.

"But here's the kicker—a series of payments from Switzerland and Panama to a Bahamian bank. They've been going on for the last three years, and that bank," she pauses, a smirk playing on her lips, "was a personal favorite of mine in my less law-abiding days."

"I'd rather not know those details, Crow. Can you track who's getting the money?"

Crow shakes her head, her hastily done ponytail swishing. "No need to track. I know who owns it. It was the Calderón gang's," she says, pinching the bridge of her nose.

"They terrorized East New York and Hunts Point. Aren't they mostly behind bars?" I ask, pointing to the screen with a confused flick of my finger.

"They had a grip on Mott Haven in the Bronx too, and yeah, almost all the big shots have been locked up for a year at least," she confirms, nodding slowly. "As for the current payouts, it could mean a couple of things. Something big paid off in installments—hits, major drug runs...or," she lets out a long sigh.

"Or what?"

"They might be regrouping," she murmurs, almost as if saying it out loud could make it real.

"Why do you know the account number for a violent gang in the Bahamas?"

Crow hesitates, biting her lower lip, like she's weighing how much truth to spill. "Let's just say we had a...difference of opinion back then," she cryptically offers.

"After all the rules I'm breaking for this investigation, I think you can trust me," I protest, my heart racing at the thought of being this close to her secrets.

"Okay, fine, but no judging," Crow sighs, rolling her eyes and leaning back with a stretch that cracks her knuckles. "After you oh-so-graciously tossed me in the slammer, a buddy of mine did a job for them that went south. Long story short, she vanished, and she meant a lot to me," she confesses, her gaze dropping to the floor.

"Did they... did they kill her?"

"The word is, by the time they found her body, she was barely recognizable. They... they did horrible things to her, raped her, cut her up while she was still alive. Those bastards," she mutters, clicking her tongue in disgust and looking away.

"And when you say you had a 'difference of opinion' with them, you mean?"

"I cut a deal with the DA for a shorter sentence in exchange for intel. Yeah, I'm not proud, but those bastards are better off behind bars. It was the only way to get back at them for my friend, from my cell."

"And shave some time off your sentence, too," I add, raising an eyebrow.

"Less time than promised," Crow complains, pulling a face. "Listen, only two people know this. Fuck, I don't even know why I'm telling you. If this gets out, I'm worse than dead."

"You can trust me," I whisper, softly tracing her back.

"Don't go getting all mushy on me, detective. My walls are a little low today," she jokes, tossing her head back with a smile that just about knocks me over.

"Do you think they're behind the murders? Trying to pin it on you?" I push, a shiver crawling up my spine.

"I guess if it was them, I'd be dead already. Whoever it is, they're trying to lock me up. Or maybe they've gone soft," she says, half-smiling.

"I don't know how you can stay so calm."

"In my old line of work, it usually ended with death or prison, detective. But seriously, I'm not calm. If they've regrouped and they know it was me, I better vanish off the face of the earth," Crow admits, suddenly looking very serious.

"Now I've got to figure out how to get a warrant to search Rummage's system without admitting we hacked him. Maybe if we take another look, we'll find something else," I suggest.

"I know a guy, Leon, one of the few who dodged the cell. He's pretty straight-up. He was low on the totem pole and didn't like how the bosses operated. Maybe I could talk to him, get some info. He's got a little shop on Staten Island."

I shake my head slowly, a wave of unease trickling down my spine. The idea doesn't sit right with me. The less I deal with those types, the better. I get her reasons; she had to avenge her friend. But the way she said it, there was definitely more to it, more than she's letting on.

I can even wrap my head around her striking a deal to shave time off her sentence in exchange for turning in those lowlifes. The streets of New York are safer without them. But letting her risk her neck like that? Only if we're out of all other options.

"I love it when you go all protective, detective," Crow teases, leaving her computer to nudge me gently back into the chair. "I could get used to someone watching out for me."

***

That night, squeezed into the tiny safe house bed, the heat pooling in my lower belly becomes unbearable. Every accidental brush of our bodies sends electric jolts through me. I feel her foot graze mine under the sheets, and she lets out a soft sigh. Then, she turns to look at me, and the air between us crackles with tension.

We just lie there for an eternity, eyes locked. Crow reaches out, her fingertips grazing my cheek, and I close my eyes, tilting my head into her touch, almost purring, I swear. Crow smiles, and our lips meet in a kiss that's all softness and warmth.

"Nobody can find out about this," I whisper, anxiety threading through my voice.

She grins again, shaking her head with an amused twinkle in her eyes before replying, "Looks like you've broken more laws today than in

107

your whole life. What's one more?" And then her lips are on mine again.

Her hand trails down my neck, then glides over the curve of my collarbone with a touch so gentle, my whole body trembles. When her hand slips under my shirt, I can't help the little moan that escapes.

As she kisses me, her fingers brush my nipples, hardening them, while my hand slides under her pajama pants. She closes her eyes, purring against my lips as my fingers find her sex, and I know the line I've crossed is indelible.

Making love that night, I realize it's different. It's not the raw, almost savage passion of our first time. There's something more, a connection that runs deeper between us.

After a wonderful climax, with her head resting on my chest and my fingers combing through her hair, Crow looks up at me, her eyes a mix of surprise and something undefinable. It's like a storm of emotions is swirling in those blue eyes.

"You know this is dangerous, right?" I sigh, breaking the stillness of the night.

"I know," Crow whispers, kissing my nipple with a tenderness that sends shivers through me, "but I don't want to stop."

Chapter 18

Crow

I blink my eyes open, and the first thing that greets me is Isabella's peaceful, sleeping face right beside me. I can't help but grin like an idiot. Tough as nails Crow, falling for the detective who once slapped cuffs on her wrists. How the heart makes fools of us all.

She's a picture of serenity, dark hair fanned out on the pillow, lips slightly parted. Beautiful. The sheet lies forgotten at her waist – she'd complained about the heat last night – and my heart does a few somersaults just taking in the sight of her bare chest.

"Good morning," I whisper, kissing her forehead, my fingertips skating over the line of her jaw.

Half asleep, Isabella purrs, seizing my hand and pressing it to her lips, igniting all my senses with that simple gesture.

"We should get moving," I remind her. "It's our last day to snoop around on our own."

She agrees with a sleepy nod and a smile that could knock you dead, "I noticed a coffee shop from one of the windows. Looks promising. We could grab breakfast and map out our day."

Stepping outside, the cool morning air slaps us even as lazy sunlight dances between the buildings, splashing everything in gold.

The moment we enter the café, the rich scent of fresh coffee wraps around us. It's a quiet place in a neighborhood where the world's languages mingle, and no one asks questions. Two ladies chat away in Chinese, and Isabella's gaze drifts to a loud, laughing Latino family.

"This coffee beats the swill at the station," she admits, eyes closing, head tipping back as the first sip hits her taste buds.

Her hand's on the table, palm up like an invitation, and I find myself caressing it, a stupid smile on my face.

"The Calderóns, they used to run their game out of an old warehouse in East New York, right?" she asks, voice dropping to a conspiratorial hush.

My muscles tense at the mention. The Calderóns were bad news, and let's not even start on my personal history with them.

"Why are you asking?"

"Think you could find that place again?" she persists, leaning in close, her eyes sharp with intention.

"Yeah, I could," I say, hesitating, "but I don't think dropping by for a visit is on my top ten list of smart moves."

"Could be a clue there, right?" Isabella's voice is low and urgent. "Place should be deserted. Worst case, we check the joint from the outside. See any action, we bail. With motorcycle helmets, no one's

110

gonna make us." She's throwing ideas like darts, each one hitting closer to the bullseye. "Easy getaway, too, on the bike." She adds.

I swirl my coffee, the spoon clinking against the mug like a judge's gavel — reluctant. I know she's got a point, but that warehouse? It's like an old wound, and digging into it... well, let's just say it's not how I'd choose to spend a sunny morning. It's where they played judge and jury, their twisted version. Where my friend suffered things I can barely let myself imagine.

"Hey, if you're not OK with it, we skip it," Isabella says, her hand finding mine, squeezing it like a lifeline. "Just thought it might be worth a quick look."

I let out a sigh; our fingers lace together like they're made for it. "Fine. A quick look. Anything smells off, we're outta there so fast they'll feel the breeze," I tell her, the 'tough as nails' persona I wear slipping just a bit.

Half an hour later, we're ditching the bike by the rusted metal fence that wraps the Calderón's old haunt. Killing the engine, I'm hit with a wave of... something. It's not fear, not exactly. The broken windows stare like dead eyes, graffiti screaming silent stories.

"We're in this together," Isabella whispers, her touch feather-light against the small of my back.

Checking for any sign of life, I pick the lock — old skills don't rust. We step into a ballet of dust motes, twirling in shafts of light slicing through the busted windows. The Calderón's den, once alive with the worst kind of energy, now just a ghostly shell; cold, empty, dead.

Flicking on her flashlight, Isabella grabs my hand, and we're wandering through the abandoned rooms. It's like she's trying to say, 'Hey, those Calderón goons? They're just bad memories rotting in a cell. But me? I'm here. I'm real.'

Her light dances over peeling paint, rusty pipes, trash piled in corners like grotesque art installations. The air is heavy with the stench of mold and rot.

We reach one brother's office — the one I stepped into once, that's it. The tables are overturned, yellowed papers scattered like afterthoughts. The place is eerily still, frozen in time. No recent activity, just decay.

Then, a noise to our right has us jumping, hearts racing. But it's just a huge rat, its presence as unwelcome as ours.

"Holy shit, nearly gave me a heart attack," Isabella mutters, her hand instinctively going for her gun.

Down a dark hallway, her light finds a door ajar. Isabella nudges it open, and there, a desk with papers — too neat, too recent. Somebody's been here.

"Fuck, Crow!" Isabella breathes out, her grip on my hand tight enough to dig her nails into my skin.

On the grimy wall, a collage — mostly snaps of me, a list of names, dates. And there's the first victim, playing with his kid, a moment frozen just days before he was killed.

I swallow the lump in my throat, trying to keep the ghosts at bay, and Isabella's hand in mine feels like the only real thing in this whole forsaken place.

Chapter 19

Isabella

"Crow, this means the Calderóns are back in action, and they're after you," I mutter, a tremor running through my body like a subway train.

Crow peers at the photographs, her brow furrowed in skepticism. "Look, all the big bosses are behind bars. The few left on the streets are just pawns; they don't have the brains to pull this off."

"They could be plotting revenge from their cells," I remind her.

"If they wanted me dead or to snatch me for a torturing session, they would've done it by now. I'm not exactly hiding out. This doesn't add up," she says, her voice calm. "The Calderóns were bloody, not brainy. Whoever's behind this is calculating, strategic. They want to see me locked up, not dead. And they're getting their kicks making me squirm, playing some sick game of chess," she sighs, the sound heavy and drawn out.

Crow stands there, rooted in front of the wall, as if the photos might start whispering secrets. She could be onto something. Someone's definitely got it in for her. But who? And why?

"Izzy, I know you hate this, but we need to talk to León," she blurts out.

***

The neon sign casts an eerie glow over the garage entrance as we hit Staten Island. Beyond a rusted metal fence, two mechanics are elbows deep in a car that's seen better days. The place smells more like a junk-yard than a repair shop.

"There he is," Crow mutters, jutting her chin toward a hulk of a man with a bandana wrapped around his head. "The big guy in the back."

"He's huge."

"I got this, Izzy," she says. "Known him forever, and we've never crossed wires. Stick close and keep your lips zipped. Especially about the whole cop thing."

He doesn't exactly scream 'trustworthy' to me. I lean in, whispering, "Are we sure about him?"

She shakes her head, quick and decisive. "Not in the slightest."

We walk past, the mechanics throwing us bored glances before re-turning to their jobs. León, the big guy, looks up, eyes wide as saucers, wiping his greasy hands on his pants like he's trying to erase evidence.

"No fucking way! Crow, back from the dead," he bellows, shaking his head in disbelief. "And your little friend here is...?"

"Just a friend," Crow clips back, dry as the desert.

"How long's it been? What brings you by? Thought you were still boxed up. Didn't you get a twelve-year sentence?" His eyes are all question marks.

"I was on my best behavior," Crow says with a shrug, her smirk telling a different story. "We need to chat... privately."

León hesitates, then jerks his head, signaling us to follow him into an office that's as dirty as his pants. He plants his massive arms over his chest like he's bracing for a storm.

"Shit, never thought I'd see you breathing. You're one tough bitch," he says, almost like he's happy to see her.

"I need the lowdown on the Calderóns," Crow cuts to the chase, no pleasantries necessary.

"Those psychos?" He spits on the floor like he's trying to poison the ground. "I'm legit now. No more trouble for me."

"And those VINs you're scrubbing? That Porsche hiding in the corner, it headed to Europe?" Crow's gaze is sharp, pointing with her chin.

"It's just some Italian business. I'd rather stay out of it. The job's simple, almost completely above board," he says, hands spread wide like he's trying to excuse himself.

"But it seems like someone's got it out for me, León," Crow pushes, her voice edged with steel. "Thought you might know why, given our... history."

León chuckles. "I can think of a few who'd want to," he jokes. "But not the Calderóns. They're all locked up, a tight operation, like someone gave the cops a cheat sheet. Those of us not behind bars? We want nothing to do with that bloodthirsty crew," he adds.

"Thanks, you've always been straight with me," Crow says, giving his arm a playful jab.

"Take care of yourself! Keep your eyes peeled. Oh, and if you've got a car that needs fixing, you know where to find me. Italian ventures are good, but a little extra cash wouldn't hurt. Times are tough," he reminds her before we say goodbye.

Stepping out of the garage, the sky has turned a murky gray, the first lazy raindrops kissing the pavement.

"Back to square one," Crow sighs, wiping down the motorcycle seat before swinging a leg over.

"We'll catch that bastard, Crow. Just watch," I whisper, sliding in behind her, my arms encircling her waist.

***

The moment we bust into the safe house, Crow's all over the computer like it's her lifeline. She's got this look like she's home when she types on a keyboard.

"What are you hunting for?" I ask, sliding up next to her.

"If it's not the Calderóns, someone's seriously got it in for me," she admits.

"Kinda glad it's not the Calderóns, though," I muse. "Assuming we can trust that guy. But earlier, I was thinking, the person behind this has got to be some tech wizard or not flying solo. Maybe another hacker?"

"Hackers don't usually go for blood," she points out.

"Yeah, but revenge? It can push people over the edge," I remind her.

"I don't know, Izzy. This whole thing is crap. Feels like we're running in place," she complains.

Outside, the wind's having a tantrum, throwing sheets of rain against the windows, and thunder growls like it's trying to shake the walls down. The trees are doing this wild dance, shadows thrashing with every gust.

"Looks like the weather's caught some Calderón fever," Crow jokes, collapsing beside me on the couch.

"Come here," I suggest, straddling her lap to kill some time before sleep claims us.

With a smirk that's all kinds of trouble, she slips her hands under my shirt, unhooking my bra like she's done it a million times. Her fingers, gentle yet deliberate, trace over my skin, thumbs grazing just so, and I'm letting out these soft moans that mingle with her breath.

"Fuck, no way!" she barks as her phone rings.

"Do you have to check it now?" I groan.

"How many people have this number?"

"Shit," I mutter while she stares at the phone like it's a snake.

"It's from that jerk."

"What's it say?"

"It's a battle to destroy the mind of your opponent," she whispers, reading it.

"Means anything to you?"

"It's a Kasparov quote. 'Chess is a battle to destroy the mind of your opponent.' He's playing games with us," Crow growls, her face twisting in disgust.

Chapter 20

Crow

The glass door to the cybercrimes unit whooshes open with a whisper, and a blast of chilled air smacks us as we step inside. Shelly looks up from the monitors and breaks into a wide grin.

"It's like a dang freezer in here," Isabella huffs, rubbing her arms for warmth.

Shelly squints at her, a mock glare taking shape. "How many times have I told you why we keep it at a frosty sixty degrees in here?" She turns to me with a roll of her eyes. "Maybe you can remind her later, though I bet she'll forget again," she teases, a smirk playing at the corner of her lips.

Isabella's all business, though. "Crow got a message on her phone—from a number very few people have. We need your tech magic, Shelly. And your vault-like discretion," she says, her voice dropping to a serious whisper. "There's a short list of people I trust these days, and it's getting shorter by the hour."

"So, your secret admirer's now into sending love notes, huh, Crow?" Shelly quips, her fingers already dancing across the keyboard.

"It's more like hate mail from the Grim Reaper," I snark back.

"Can you trace the call or not?" Isabella's impatience is as palpable as the cold.

"Calm down, detective. We're on it," Shelly says, her eyes never leaving the screen. "This won't be a walk in the park, right, Crow?"

I nod. The guy behind this knows his stuff, or he's got a hacker wizard on speed dial. Even with our lab tricks and tech voodoo, I doubt we'll pin down that message. And Shelly's aware, her brow furrowed in concentration.

"This creep's slick," she mutters, the screen awash with cascading code walls. "It's routed through a maze of proxies across different countries, masking the real source."

"I bet they're using a false trail too, bouncing the signal through burner phones before it hits home base," I add. "This guy's going to great lengths to stay off the radar."

Isabella sighs, the frustration crackling around us like static. Shelly, though, she's eating up our tech talk like it's her favorite dish.

"Seems like prison didn't dull your criminal instincts," she says with a wink. "But hey, if you ever tire of playing tag with Detective No-Fun here, maybe I could snag you a gig with us."

"She's a bit of a stick in the mud, but she grows on you," I joke, nodding toward Isabella. "Still, I can't deny I'd love to get my hands on all the toys and computing power you guys got here. Imagine that, detective? Hacking from within the cybercrimes unit itself? Man, that'd be the dream."

"Or, maybe you could go legit and help us catch the bad guys," Shelly adds with a shrug.

I don't reply, but I'm pretty sure a goofy smile makes its way onto my lips. Me, working as a consultant for the cybercrimes unit? I've got to admit, the idea isn't half-bad.

"If you ever get tired of playing nanny to Detective Alvarez, come find me. Given your history, I might have to sweet-talk Chief Davis, but my offer stands," she says. But before I can consider it further, Isabella grabs my elbow and steers me out of the room in a hurry.

Back in her office, there's a storm brewing in Detective Alvarez's eyes. Maybe she's pissed about hitting a wall with the call. "Could've told you that," I would've said if she asked.

"You seem to get along with Shelly pretty well."

"She's smart," I admit. "And she actually appreciates my skills, unlike some," I add, reaching over to playfully nudge her shoulder.

"Would you take the job if they offered it to you?"

"Jealous?"

"Quit the bullshit and let's get back to work," she snaps, laying out the case clues on her desk like a macabre deck of cards.

Her brusque reaction stings. I thought she'd be happy for me, maybe even excited about the prospect of me going straight, working in the same building.

The victims' faces stare back at us from the table, their eyes etched with the terror of meeting death. They're just pawns, random sacrifices in a sadistic game, a murderer's egocentric gambit.

I should feel something more. Maybe rage for their senseless deaths. Perhaps sorrow for their cut-short stories. Instead, there's this eerie emptiness.

"What's on your mind? Talk to me, Crow, what's bothering you?" Isabella's voice pulls me back, and I think it's time to be real with her.

"Look, I don't know how to tell you about this, and I'm kicking myself for not bringing it up before," I start off slow, weighing my words like they're gold on a scale. "That Calderón family case... wasn't the only scoop I passed to the DA's office that ended with handcuffs," I confess, exhaling a sigh so heavy it could've carried my secrets with it.

Isabella freezes, her gaze fixed on me, bewildered, a pen locked in her grip like she's about to snap it in two.

"What the hell are you talking about, Crow?" she presses, her voice dropping an octave.

"Well, it's not like I made a habit of it, okay? And for the record, I wasn't in it for gain, just... dealing out justice and—"

"Can you just focus for once?" Isabella explodes, slapping the desk so hard the papers jump like they're scared, too.

"Alright, alright... geez, touchy much?" I shoot back. "There were these cases, see, where some lowlifes took advantage of the little guys and the cops... well, they couldn't cut it. So, let's just say, 'allegedly', I slipped some incriminating details to the DA. Totally anonymous, 'allegedly'. Not confirming or denying."

"And those people, they ended up behind bars?"

"Yeah," I murmur.

"Now you tell me?"

"And if you keep this up, I won't spill another word. You seemed so chill earlier. Get that I wasn't sure if I could trust you. You didn't trust me either, so holding back some intel is normal. Besides, you probably wouldn't get my reasons."

Isabella goes quiet, her jaw clenched tight as a drum. I brace for another burst of fury, another smack on the desk, but she leaves me cold with her comeback.

"You're right. I don't get it," she growls. "You have no clue what it's like to be a cop, chasing shadows in a double homicide. You don't know what it's like laying awake, wondering if you're the next target while you're hoarding crucial case intel. And all because you're unsure if you can trust me after we've... after we've been fucking."

"Hey, I've helped lock up some real monsters. Scum that would still be walking free. It's just... the timing never seemed right to tell you. We've had quite the emotional rollercoaster these past few days."

"It's not your call!" Isabella yells. "Who the fuck do you think you are, playing judge? What makes you think you're worthy to decide who goes to jail and who doesn't?"

"I was just trying to help the only way I knew how," I sigh.

"You're an idiot, damn it!" Isabella snaps, her voice biting like a winter chill in New York. She waves me off with a flip of her hand, disgust etched in every line of her face. "I should've known better than to trust you. Guess some things never change. You'll always be a crook," she adds, her disdain clear in her gaze.

"Go to hell," I mutter, my words as sharp as the icy wind whipping down the city streets. I storm out of her office, slamming the door a little harder than necessary.

I stride out of the building, my face a mask of cool indifference. I don't let anyone see the moisture in my eyes, but Isabella's words sting like salt on a raw wound. I wander the city streets aimlessly, a blur of faces and honking taxis swimming around me.

At some random corner, I stop and lean against a wall, my breath forming clouds in the cold air. I slam my hand against the bricks, once, twice, letting out a muffled scream, a mix of anger and frustration. It echoes off the concrete, lost in the city's cacophony.

She judges me by my past, like a shadow I can't shake. In her eyes, I've never stopped being a criminal, even now, when I've tried to do some good, put bad guys behind bars where they belong.

Suddenly, the truth seeps into my bones, cold and heavy. I let myself dream of a different future, something good for once in my life, but I can't escape from a past brimming with thorns. I never stood a real chance, did I? Our worlds are too different, linked by nothing more than the occasional sex.

Did I actually think we could have something real? What a joke.

I'm a fool. She's got to maintain her perfect detective image, pristine and unblemished. And yet, waking up beside her felt so right, so... beautiful.

Chapter 21

Isabella

I pace the sidewalk, feeling like a caged animal, emotions clawing at me with no escape. Yesterday, I let loose words meant only to wound. Hurt that I didn't know sooner, jealous of the bond blooming between Shelly and Crow, but today, I'm drowning in regret. I called her a crook when all she's done is help our case from the start.

The sadness in her eyes, the disappointment... it's too much to bear. Those words should've never passed my lips. I didn't mean them. And the worst part? Now that I've pushed Crow away, I'm starting to realize just how much I've fallen for her.

Standing at her door, I clutch the box of chocolates like a lifeline, praying she won't chuck it right back at me.

"What the fuck do you want?" she barks as the door swings open.

"Can we talk?" I ask, my voice shaky, lifting the box almost like a shield.

She doesn't say a word but steps aside to let me in, at least.

We sink onto a sun-cracked sofa. It's my first time inside her apartment, and it's a hot mess. Take-out boxes not yet tossed, origami roses everywhere. I fiddle with the ribbon on the chocolates, searching for the right words to shatter this awful silence.

"You've been busy, huh?" I say, trying to sound casual as I nod at the roses. God, that sounded lame.

"It helps with the stress. Started making them in prison," she says.

"Listen, Crow," I sigh, "I'm so sorry about yesterday. I shouldn't have said those things. You know I don't mean them, I just..."

"A bit late for apologies, detective. You said them, and that's what counts."

"Damn it, Crow. I really am sorry," I confess, blinking fast to fend off the tears.

"You made me feel worthless yesterday, like I meant nothing to you. You can't imagine how much that hurt," she says softly, her stunning blue eyes piercing through me.

"I've been up all night thinking about it. If I could turn back time, I'd slap some sense into myself," I admit, letting out a long breath and reaching for her hand, hoping she doesn't pull away.

Crow turns my hand over and traces delicate, imaginary patterns on my palm. It's like she's writing an apology in her own way, and my heart races at the contact.

"You've built more walls around your heart than I ever could," she states, shaking her head in disbelief.

"Crow, I'm... damn it, I'm falling for you," the words tumble out of my mouth, and I'm just as shocked as she is to hear them.

Her eyebrow arches in surprise, and for a split second, I can't tell if she's about to slap me or pull me into a kiss. She does neither.

"What?" she asks, clearly thrown off.

"Shit, Crow. I can't help it. This isn't just about sex, or just feeling comfortable around you... it's... damn, I actually feel something for you," I sigh, my lip caught between my teeth.

The shock that sketched itself across her face softens. She leans in close, careful as if approaching a skittish kitten. Her hands cradle my face, her thumb sweeping away a tear I didn't even realize had escaped.

"Never thought I'd see the day the tough detective would cry," she teases with a hiss.

"I cried all night," I confess.

"Don't sweat it. Your secret's safe with me. I won't ruin your rep as the hard-nosed cop," she jokes.

"You're ridiculous," I chuckle nervously, pulling her into a hug that feels like coming home.

As we part, I muster the courage to say the words I never imagined I'd let out.

"I love you, Angie."

The sentence hangs there, heavy in the air. I even used her real name, the one she holds close. She just looks at me, and for a heart-stopping moment, I'm scared I've made a colossal mistake.

"Wow," she finally breathes out, her eyebrows lifting.

Crow reaches out, tucking a stray lock of hair behind my ear with a gentle touch.

"I know this can't be easy, but I want to try. Maybe after the case wraps up and..." Emotions choke off my words.

"Let's take it one step at a time, detective," she whispers, tapping the tip of my nose. "Before getting all romantic, we've got a killer to catch, remember?"

I nod. "List everyone you've flipped to the justice system, will you?" I watch her, hoping for a short registry.

Her pen scratches across the paper, the bittersweet symphony of our current truce. Spilling my guts, telling her I love her, it was like jumping without a net. My heart raced hearing the words echo between us, but she—she didn't echo them back. No sweet echo, no embrace, not even a kiss. Just a quirky tap on the nose that left me more puzzled than comforted.

"There, done! Wow, that's a longer list than I thought," she exclaims, handing it over.

I pore over the list. Most are behind bars, or not worth a second glance. Some have met their maker. That's the price of screwing over a ton of people.

Then, a name leaps off the page.

"Wayne Collins," I mutter under my breath.

"Talk about awkward. There I was in jail, having to testify against him because of you, detective," she points at me, her finger accusing yet playful. "If you'd given me a couple more hours, I could've covered my tracks. But no, you had to slap the cuffs on."

"You know they let him out recently, right?"

She snorts. "Must've been his fancy friends. Always a pompous ass. But there's a difference between messing up lives in the slums and killing for revenge," she muses, her sarcasm not quite masking her concern.

"Just like him, thinking he can toy with us while getting his revenge. He always thought he was above the law," I remind her.

Wayne Collins once had it all—power, prestige, high-level contacts, and more cash than sense. Crow's testimony helped topple his empire. If anyone's got a vendetta against Crow, it's him.

"I still can't believe the judge threw out the videos of his... escapades with minors. Disgusting," she spits out.

Chapter 22

Isabella

Tracking down Collins' last known address lands me in front of an apartment block nestled in a modest slice of the city. A far cry from the glossy skyscraper where he used to lord over his empire.

His lips twist into a smirk at the sight of us, and my blood simmers. Down on his luck or not, the stench of his arrogance hangs in the air like thick smoke. He's still the same narcissist who thinks he's untouchable, perched high above us mere mortals.

"What brings you to my humble abode, Detective Alvarez?" Collins drawls.

He leans back in his chair, hands clasped behind his neck in a cocky display. He eyes Crow with a sneer, ignoring her presence. I just hold his gaze, hoping to rattle him.

"As you're well aware, I've served my time. Unjustly, I might add, but I'm square with the law now," he states.

I keep my cool, sliding the case file across the table, scattering gruesome photos to gauge his reaction.

"Look familiar, Collins?" I ask, my finger hovering over the Black Baracca rose left beside the body.

"Should it, detective? Floral arrangements aren't exactly my forte, unlike that street rat over there," he retorts, shrugging off the implication with infuriating ease and pointing to Crow.

She jumps in, "Pissed you went to prison because of me, and now you're trying to pin two murders on me?" She's revealing more than she ought to.

"Yeah, it sucked, losing everything to your little moral crusade, but wandering around killing people and leaving pretty flowers? Not my style. I'm not that in touch with my feminine side."

I glance over at the chessboard on his desk, "Nice chess set, Collins. Looks expensive," I comment, noting the beautifully carved wood pieces positioned prominently. "I'd hope you wouldn't think of starting a game with human lives at stake."

"Chess is quite stimulating," he responds, dismissing my insinuation with a wave of his hand.

"Crow chimes in. "There are lots of books about Garry Kasparov. 'How Life Imitates Chess'... big fan of the grandmaster?"

He smiles, "I appreciate a strategic mind, and his is certainly exceptional."

His composure doesn't falter. When he speaks again, his voice is dangerously smooth.

"I get this hunch you've got nothing on me, Detective, am I right?" He arches an eyebrow at me, a smirk playing on his lips like he's just caught the scent of victory. "Excuse me, but this little chat of ours is over. Next time you wanna talk, I'd appreciate it if that, um, tattooed street rat wasn't here," he says, flicking his chin toward Crow, his tongue clicking in distaste as if he's just bitten into something sour.

He smooths his tie, that self-satisfied grin stretching across his face. The guy thinks he's scored a point today, but I'm not about to let him off the hook that easily, even if my hands are tied without any evidence to pin him down just yet. His pride is going to be his downfall. I can feel it in my bones.

***

"I'm going to nail that jerk to the wall if it's the last thing I do," Crow growls as we stride out of the building, her voice biting the chilly New York air.

"Hey, we've got nothing. Not even circumstantial evidence," I remind her, feeling the weight of our empty hands.

"What about that Kasparov quote?" she throws back at me.

"You want me to get an arrest warrant because the guy admires Kasparov? Really?" I scoff. "Forget it, Crow. We'll keep digging, turn over every stone, and if it's him, we'll catch him. But right now, we've got zilch," I insist.

"I know," she sighs, the fire in her eyes dimming just a notch.

"How about I whip us up some dinner at my place? If you're up for it, that is," I offer, trying to lighten the mood.

"You can cook?" she asks, eyebrows raised in surprise.

"It's one of my hidden talents."

She gives me a playful wink. "I'd say you have other talents, but I won't remind you in case it goes to your head, detective," she murmurs.

Back at my apartment, I'm grateful for the distraction of cooking together. I won't admit it out loud, but after a grueling day, the intimacy of creating a meal side by side softens my heart more than I care to acknowledge.

With music setting the rhythm, and stolen kisses sprinkled in, the mundane task of chopping and dicing turns unexpectedly fun.

"You're pretty good with a knife," I say, genuinely surprised at her adeptness as she slides the knife through the vegetables on the cutting board.

"Honed my skills in prison," she quips, not looking up. "In the prison kitchen, don't get any ideas, detective," she adds, then leans over to give me a kiss, "and by the way, it smells amazing."

"Are we okay?" I ask, my voice tinged with apprehension.

She pauses, really thinks about it, and my heart stalls for a beat.

"We're good," she whispers. "But don't pull something like that again because there won't be another chance. I won't let you hurt me like that," Crow warns me, her eyes locking with mine.

Sitting at the table, the stress of the day melts away with each bite. The conversation flows, and every time she takes my hand in hers, I feel a warmth in my belly that's hard to ignore.

"Do you want to stay over?" I ask, blushing slightly as we finish dessert.

"What you said this morning about loving me..."

"Every single letter," I assure her, my heart in my throat.

Like she did this morning, she doesn't respond with words. She just nods and smiles, leaving me breathless.

"So, you'll stay?"

"Yeah, your bed beats mine," Crow jokes, shrugging nonchalantly, "but I need a shower," she says, lifting her right arm and pretending to sniff her armpit.

***

Water droplets cascade down Crow's bare skin, glistening like tiny diamonds, and I can't help but bite my lower lip as my eyes dance over her figure.

"You like what you see? 'Cause you're fucking me with your eyes," she teases, a mischievous smile playing on her lips while she cocks an eyebrow.

I roll my eyes and try to play it cool, but truth be told, I can't tear my gaze away from her naked body. Crow laughs, grabs the shampoo, and pours a liberal amount into her palm.

"Come here, turn around," she whispers, nodding her head in direction.

With my eyes closed, I let out a sigh as the scent of lavender fills the air, her hands running through my hair with a sensuality that's out of this world, massaging my scalp until I can't help but moan. Maybe it's feeling her breasts against my back or her thighs brushing my ass that makes me let out a few more moans.

"I could get used to this," I breathe out, tipping my head back.

Suddenly, her hands pause, and I open my eyes, surprised, turning to meet her intense gaze that leaves me breathless.

"Yeah?" she asks, her voice low.

I nod slowly, words failing me, and Crow leans in to kiss my neck. Then she pushes my body against the shower wall. I spread my hands wide for support while she caresses my breasts, sending jolts of pleasure down as she grinds against me, making me shiver.

"Could you get used to this?" she hisses by my ear before giving me a gentle bite on the shoulder.

"Damn, Crow," I gasp.

"Turn around," she commands.

I obey, and her eyes blaze with a primal passion. She takes my right hand and presses it against her sex, her breath hitching as she says, "Feel what you do to me."

My fingers explore her, slick with desire, and we lose ourselves in a symphony of moans and gasps that seems to stretch on forever. Beneath the shower's spray, we're lost in each other, pushing, stroking, kissing, wrapped up in limitless pleasure until Crow shudders against me, her free hand tangled in my hair as she continues to move with me.

"Please, don't stop," I beg Crow, my breath choppy, as a wave of pure bliss crashes over me. I clamp her hand against me, desperate to keep those fingers where they are, driving me wild, amplifying the pleasure that ripples through me. I'm wrapped up in kisses, full of heat and passion, muffling my moans against her lips.

She grins, that gorgeous grin of hers, and turns off the shower. With a gentleness that belies her rough exterior, Crow wraps me in a towel, pulling me close, holding me against her as if she can't bear the thought of ever letting go.

Later, snuggled against her bare skin while she softly kisses my head, her arms enveloping me, it's too easy to dream that maybe, just maybe, this could last forever.

"I love you," I whisper, kissing her nipple as she drifts off to sleep, not expecting an answer this time.

Chapter 23

Crow

"Turn that damn phone off, Izzy," I grumble, burying my head under the pillow to shut out the noise. Isabella fumbles for her phone on the nightstand, and the screen's glow washes over her face in the dark.

"Detective Isabella Alvarez," she answers, her voice scratchy and tense.

I prop myself up on one elbow, watching her. These 3 AM calls are never good news. The conversation is short, way too short. Her eyes go wide, and she stares at the now blank screen, hands shaking.

"What did they want?" I ask.

"They want me to stay away from you," she says. "It was a warning. They said you'll end up in jail or dead soon and that anyone who falls for you tends to lose their life."

"That all?" I say with a smirk.

"They also called you a bitch."

Sleep instantly evaporates. This is getting way too personal. Without a word, I snatch the cold phone from her and hook it up to my laptop.

"What are you doing?" Isabella asks, a hint of confusion in her voice.

"Trying to trace the call," I say, as if it's obvious. "I'm guessing we'll hit the same wall as at the cybercrimes lab—tracks covered nicely. Still, I want to try something new. I've mixed one of your sniffers with an exploit I cooked up and..."

"What do you mean 'one of our sniffers'? I don't even know what that is, but why 'yours'?" she cuts in, brow furrowed.

"Maybe I borrowed it from the cybercrimes unit," I mutter, trying to keep focused on the trace.

"Damn it, Crow," she sighs.

"I was planning to improve it and give it back to Shelly," I insist, throwing up my hands in defense against her stern look. Isabella shakes her head, but I swear I catch a half-smile slipping through.

The software is useless again. Whoever is behind this knows their stuff, or they're paying someone who does. Much as it pains me, I guess the washed-up, corrupt lawyer is off the suspect list.

"I'm more convinced every day that someone in my unit is behind these crimes," Isabella says, her hands pressing gently on my shoulders in a tiny, comforting massage.

The next morning, dark shadows have taken up residence under her eyes. My brain feels sluggish, too. We've slept little, and even worse. Izzy sees enemies everywhere, trusts no one—not even Shelly or Chief Davis.

"I still say if you have a mole, it's that bitch with the weird last name and the resting dog face," I grumble, taking a long sip of my coffee.

"Kalinsky?"

"Yeah, her."

"She's a fool, but she's not the type," Isabella says, her voice dropping to a whisper, her hand tenderly brushing my cheek with the back of her fingers. "Motive is the key in any crime, and her? She's got zero. Plus, knowing there's murder in the mix? Kalinsky wouldn't go that far. Right now, it feels like you're the only one I can trust."

"Wow, that's... not saying much."

"It's everything, Angie," Isabella sighs, her thumb tracing my lips softly.

"I was getting used to being Crow," I quip.

Izzy cracks a smile, but before she can throw a witty comeback, her phone rings, slicing through the moment. She winces at the caller ID before answering, "Detective Alvarez. You do know it's my day off, right, Smith?"

Her face twists, a storm cloud passing over her eyes. She glances up, lets out a long, defeated breath. "Another one? We're on our way," she responds, hanging up.

She jumps up from the table, urgency in every line of her body, and motions for me to follow. "Another victim. And guess what, they left

141

a black rose again," she tells me, tucking her gun into its holster with a swift, practiced move.

***

The stench of death greets me like an unwelcome neighbor, creeping up my nostrils before I even step foot in the apartment. This scene's got a different flavor. My eyes sweep across the living room, taking in the chaos of overturned furniture and a shattered mirror, evidence of a desperate struggle.

"A familiar face must've opened the door," the forensic tech notes, eyeing the intact lock. "No forced entry here."

That's when I see her.

My stomach knots up as if it's trying to strangle my insides. The sight of her still body on the floor hits me hard. Her eyes, once sparkling with a life that could light up the darkest alleys of New York, now dull and glassy with terror, silently screaming the story of her last moments.

"No, please, not Eva," I whisper, collapsing to my knees beside her.

Isabella reaches out, trying to lift me up. I barely feel her touch, but she gets the message when I don't budge, and she lets me be, a silent reminder to keep my hands off the crime scene.

The guy from forensics drones on with a monotonous voice, rattling off the grim checklist: blunt force trauma, signs of restraint, evidence of a fight that didn't end quick. And then there's the rose, so out of place it might as well be a punchline, nothing like the previous two murders. This woman fought back.

I'm fighting the urge to hurl, to scream, to smash something, to mourn. Instead, I listen as the tech describes a sweater folded under Eva's head like some twisted pillow, a cruel comfort offered post-mortem.

"It's like the perp cared, in a messed up way," he shrugs.

Cared? Since when does propping up a dead girl's head with a sweater after you've bashed it in count as affection?

"I'm so sorry, Eva," I murmur, unable to tear my eyes away from her lifeless gaze. Those eyes that used to drive me wild with just one of her sly grins.

Isabella's hand is gentle on my back, her touch a silent acknowledgment. She doesn't need to ask, doesn't need to judge. She just knows. There was something deep between Eva and me. And now, because of some sick twist of fate, some vendetta, her light's been snuffed out.

"That's what that damn three a.m. text was about," I growl, the anger in my voice barely contained.

And then, something inside me snaps. I let out a raw, torn scream, trying to wrap my arms around Eva, to hold her one last time, but Isabella and the tech pull me back. They're murmuring apologies, trying to be the barrier between me and the tidal wave of grief. Still, all I can think about is catching the bastard responsible.

143

"I loved her," I admit through tears, as Isabella wraps me up in a hug that feels like the only real thing in a room that's suddenly too full of cops pretending not to stare.

Talking about Eva in the past tense is like admitting she's really gone. No more laughter under the sun, no more pillow talk after making love. I begged her not to visit me in prison, to forget me, to move on without me. And now, her future's been stolen in one violent act, another pawn gone in this sick game of chess.

"Can you hold on?" Isabella asks as she clings to me tightly.

"Sorry, Izzy, I'm making a spectacle of myself at a crime scene. I'm supposed to be a consultant for the cops," I apologize, feeling every bit the fool.

She gifts me a beautiful smile, her only response. Squeezing my hand, she kisses my forehead, right when the forensic tech decides to barge in on our moment.

He guides us to the body, a black rose lying beside it like a dark omen.

"The killer left this note in the victim's hand. No prints," he informs, passing a bloodstained piece of paper to Isabella.

"It's for you."

"What's it say?" I ask, a twinge of fear in my voice.

"'Time to bring you down a peg, crow,'" she reads under her breath.

That's when it clicks, somewhere deep in my mind. Those words... those fucking words are familiar. But where?

144

I rack my brain, mentally parading past faces, and there it is. Roman Knox. The scrawny, arrogant hacker who hated to lose.

"Can you describe him?" Isabella probes.

"Tall, skinny. Greasy hair, red eyes from screen glare. He was a pompous ass, but harmless. Hopelessly in love with Eva, though she never gave him the time of day. He took our dating pretty hard, like a personal defeat," I recall with a sneer of contempt.

"That could fit our suspect."

"Izzy, did you catch the part about 'thin and harmless'? Think Scooby-Doo cartoons. He's like Shaggy, the hippy dog owner," I explain, my mouth twisting with scorn.

"You're talking about eight years ago..."

"Yeah, exactly, but still... Oh, fuck!"

"What's wrong?" she asks, her detective's confusion clear.

"Shit, I don't know. I'm hit by this wild idea, but it can't be. That guy from the charity gala... the Yacht Club one..."

"The one who punched me and knocked me to the ground?"

"Yeah, that's the one. Barely got a good look, but... shave his head, slap on a muscle mountain from eight years of gym time, throw on a hideous neck tattoo, and... No, forget it, it's crazy," I rush out, shaking my head in denial.

Chapter 24

Crow

The thought that Roman Knox might be behind Eva's murder hits me like a freight train. I scramble for a connection, but the details slip through my fingers like sand.

"It can't be," I whisper, my voice barely there.

Isabella rests her right hand on my shoulder, squeezing gently. "I know it doesn't all add up, but we must consider every angle. Tell me more about that guy," she murmurs.

"It's impossible. He was a scrawny geek. Thought he was above everyone, but he was harmless. Lived in his brother Caleb's shadow. Roman was obsessed with chess and computers. Did you know his parents named him after Roman Dzindzichashvili?"

"Who's that?"

"Never mind, he's a chess grandmaster from Georgia who later played for the U.S. He's an Excellent player. Knox's folks had high hopes for him, and he never really made it past the scholastic level. Guess that added to his frustration," I explain.

"People change, Crow. Eight years is a long time," Isabella adds softly.

"Yeah, well, with Roman, I find that hard to believe. He was the type to live in his parents' basement, glued to a computer screen day and night."

Our conversation is cut short by Detective Kalinsky striding into Isabella's office. She leans against the doorframe, arms crossed, not bothering to hide her disdain.

"Really cozying up to the criminal, huh? Still trading kisses or have you moved on to screwing?" she spits out with contempt.

"Do you need something? We're working on a case, as you know. If you can contribute, I'd appreciate it; otherwise, we'd prefer to be left alone," Isabella responds, barely keeping her cool, judging by the way her knuckles turn white, clutching the edge of the table.

"What's it like being on the other side of the law, Crow?" she sneers at my nickname like it's a curse. "Or should I say being on both sides at once?"

"It has its perks, free coffee, donuts, and I don't have to run every time I see a cop. I could get used to this life," I retort, my voice dripping with sarcasm.

Kalinsky's face turns beet red. Clearly, she was hoping to get a rise out of me, but it takes a lot more than that. Eight years behind bars train you not to take the bait.

"Well, Alvarez might buy your reformed good girl act, but you don't fool me. Once a criminal, always a criminal," she snaps before storming out of sight.

***

"You gotta see this," Shelly hollers as we step into the cyber crimes unit lab.

"Surprise us."

"We've been combing through everything on Roman Knox. Turns out, he had a brother he was tight with and—"

"Caleb, could've told you that," I cut in, "he was the charming one."

"But did you know what happened to Caleb?" Shelly presses on.

I just shrug. Eight years in the slammer have left holes in my life, like someone took an eraser to parts of my hard drive. There's before prison, and then there's after, but the middle's kinda fuzzy.

"I'm lost..."

"Caleb Knox got nabbed not long after you. They tied him to the Calderón gang bust and—"

"Holy shit," I sigh.

"Exactly. Someone leaked the dirt on those guys through an anonymous tip."

Isabella's hand creases her forehead, and she lets out this long sigh that seems to carry the world's weight. She looks at me like she's saying, "look at the can of worms your anonymous tips have opened."

"Craziest part? Caleb was only facing two years, but he ended up dying in jail under, let's say, 'fishy' circumstances."

"By 'fishy,' you mean...?" Isabella jumps in.

"Stabbed in the restroom. Of course, nobody saw or heard a thing. He was gone before hitting the hospital. Word on the street is the Calderóns thought he'd been chatting with the cops," explains Shelly.

"Jesus," I breathe out, collapsing into a chair and burying my face in my hands.

"It's not on you," Isabella whispers, her hand tracing comforting circles on my back, "You did the right thing, keeping that trash off the streets. No way you could've known the Calderóns would pin it on him," she adds, after Shelly wanders off for a Coke.

"Do you think Roman blames me for his brother's death?" I ask, fear knotting up in my throat.

"Sure as hell sounds like a solid motive for revenge," the detective pipes up.

"Fuck," I mutter under my breath.

"Hey, you put away a dangerous gang, took 'em off the streets. You made the world a bit better. It's not on you that things went south for Caleb Knox," she reminds me.

149

"Or for Eva," I sigh out.

I nod slowly, but her words can't shake the guilt twisting in my gut. No matter how righteous my reasons, my actions ended in tragedy. I'm broken, been that way since I was a kid, and misfortune seems to follow me wherever I go.

"The only one to blame is the murderer," Shelly chimes in, cracking open her can of Coke.

"We need to stop Roman," I declare, springing from my chair with a jolt.

"If only it were that simple. He's vanished off the face of the earth."

"I know this is huge for you, Angie. We'll get justice, catch that bastard, I promise," Isabella says, leaning in to kiss my head, not caring one bit about Shelly's quizzical stare - or maybe that's exactly why.

My heart races at the thought. Is she sending a message to our tech wizard? Because that kiss seemed to scream, "Back off, Shelly, Crow's taken." Izzy doesn't realize how much that possessive move just turned me on.

While Shelly and Isabella pore over Caleb's case, an alert on the monitor snags my attention. Someone's digging into the same file. I frown; this case has been cold for years. Who else would be prying into it? But when I check the account that's made the inquiry, my jaw hits the floor.

"I'm gonna grab a sandwich, be right back. I'm starving," I lie, darting out the door.

I sprint down the hallway to the office, my heart pounding so hard it feels like it's trying to punch its way out of my ribcage. Kalinsky's got her eyes on me the second I burst in, looking all kinds of puzzled.

"What do you want?" she spits, her voice dripping with venom.

"Just curious," I say, trying to sound casual, "Why're you digging into the Caleb Knox case? It's been closed for ages."

"What makes you think I'm interested? Don't you have anything better to do? Why don't you go down on Alvarez's and leave me alone?"

I can't help but smirk. "The magical elves living in the servers casually mentioned it. Thought it was odd you'd request the file, but hey, they're just magical elves, not cops. They live in the cyber realm."

"Are you stupid? Spying on me now? I'm gonna complain to Chief Davis so fast, you and Alvarez will wish you never crossed me," Kalinsky snarls, slapping a hand down on the desk.

For a second, I'm tempted to push her buttons some more, but I don't wanna drag Izzy into a mess. I'll play it cool until I figure out why this woman seems to hate my guts.

"Alright, alright, I was just bored, wandering the halls. Since I'm on this provisional release thing, I'm not allowed to do much. I'll leave you to it."

151

"Wait!" she yells.

"You talking to me?"

"Yeah, of course, I'm talking to you. Since you know so much, why has Alvarez pulled the same file?" That direct hit throws me for a loop, but now I'm on high alert.

"No clue. You know, she does her own thing, doesn't tell me much. We chat, that's about it. Chief Davis's orders. Alvarez didn't want me on the case. Now she keeps me around for my charming personality and my skills in... you know..."

I pause, flicking my tongue in a mock ice cream-licking gesture, and Kalinsky scoffs with a look that's a mix of disgust and something else I can't quite place.

As I head back to the cyber crimes unit, I'm rehearsing the perfect words to spill to Isabella about my little discovery. Izzy's gonna have my head, but whatever Kalinsky's interest is in Roman's brother, it's nothing but trouble for us.

***

"We need to talk," I blurt out the moment we hit her apartment.

I'd decided to wait until she'd left the cyber crimes unit. I mean, I trust Shelly, like 99.9%, but I figure, why not play it safe? One wrong move, and everything goes to hell.

"You've been chatting with Kalinsky behind my back?" Isabella throws me this look of pure disbelief when I spill about my chat with the detective.

"If you don't find it sketchy that she's suddenly all up in the Kaleb Knox case now, then I don't know what to tell you," I shoot back.

"Yeah, it's suspicious," she concedes.

"Should we tell Chief Davis?"

"I don't know who to trust," Isabella sighs.

"I'm telling you, Kalinsky's the mole in your department," I push on.

"I can't just accuse a colleague without cause. Right now, you're the only one I trust, Angie. With my career, my life even."

I hate to show weakness, but I joke, "You're gonna make me cry," trying to play it off, but hiding my feelings around her is getting tougher by the second.

"I gotta admit, your wild theories about Detective Kalinsky are starting to seem more legit. But I can't see the connection between her and Roman Knox."

"Wild theories?" I feign outrage, hand to heart. "Let me just hack her computer. It'll be a piece of cake. She won't even notice."

Isabella closes her eyes, shaking her head, but I can tell she's amused. Then she slips her hand under my belt, pulling me close for a kiss that wipes my mind clean of killers and moles for a blissful moment.

153

"Angie, right now, you mean everything to me. And I'm not just talking about some romantic or sexual attraction. You're my partner in this case. I know you'd do anything to protect me, and I'd do the same for you. But I can't let you hack a cop's computer," she says, her lips brushing the tip of my nose.

I'm grinning like an idiot, especially hearing my name on her lips. After Eva's death, she's the only one who uses it. To everyone else, I'm Crow, the hacker, the criminal. They think Angie died long ago on the tough city streets as a kid, leaving a thief in her place. Only Izzy sees the real me, behind the tattoos and the tough-as-nails act.

"You know I'm not exactly Miss Trustworthy, right?" I warn her. "I mean, my past's kind of checkered for you to be putting this much faith in me."

"Look at me, Angie," she whispers, slipping two fingers under my chin to tilt my face up, her touch sending a shiver down my spine. "I mean every word I've said. I want to be with you, now and after this case wraps up. But only if you want it too, if you're really sure."

Her voice falters, uncertain. She bites her lower lip, hesitating, and I swear my heart is about to pound out of my chest any second now.

"I want this," she continues, her hand finding mine, thumb gently skating over my knuckles. "I want you."

"Izzy," I start, every word heavy, "my whole life has been about just making it through the day. I don't do relationships. I'm broken, completely. And the worst part? I tend to break everything I touch,

154

which is why I never let anyone get too close. I'm scared it'll all end up a disaster."

"That's not going to happen," she insists.

"But you... you make me believe that I deserve more than what I've had. That I deserve to be happy. Maybe it's just a fantasy, but it's a pretty damn beautiful one," I confess, a raw edge to my voice.

"You do deserve it, Angie," Isabella says, sealing her promise with a kiss that makes every doubt evaporate for the moment.

And that night, curled up next to her warm, bare skin, I let myself dream of a different life. A life where I'm not Crow, the criminal, but Angie Hollander, computer expert, consultant for the NYPD, monster hunter.

That night, I dream of a little house just outside the city. It's got a tiny yard and a white picket fence. A dog darts around in front of us while we laugh, maybe chased by one or two kids.

In my dream, I allow myself happiness. Tomorrow, when I wake up, I'll be Crow again. Broken inside, raised on the streets. The one who's too scared to say "I love you" out of fear it'll all vanish.

Chapter 25

Isabella

"I might die tomorrow," I mutter, gnawing on the inside of my lip so hard I can taste blood on my tongue. Panic creeps in as I start to digest the stark reality of our plan.

"Detective, you're going sheet white," Crow tries to jest, yet her hands quiver over the keyboard like leaves in a storm.

"Listen, Isabella," Shelly cuts in, her hand landing on my shoulder with a gentle squeeze. "I know it's scary, but we've got this under control, okay?"

"As much control as you can have over a wild card," Crow adds, cranking up my nerves even more.

My desire to nab that jerk Roman Knox has me nodding like a bobblehead, blind and foolhardy. Crow's plan is risky, borderline idiotic. Utter madness. As a cop, I know better than just crossing my fingers and hoping it all works out. Yet here I am, gambling my life.

"See it this way," her whisper slices through my racing thoughts. "If I don't take the job, someone else will. And then, it'll be a whole lot more dangerous."

Ever since we caught Jeremy Bennett, Shelly's been monitoring that Dark Web forum where Roman hired him. Yesterday, one name set off our alarms: "Isabella Alvarez."

Someone's put a price on my head. And according to Crow, they're willing to pay top dollar.

The thought of my life being worth any amount of money makes me want to hurl. And I mean, literally, puke my guts out.

"Damn, I look evil," Crow blurts, flashing me an AI-altered photo where she's dolled up like a hitwoman with a resume full of violent crime.

Shelly and I have definitely crossed a line into the iffy side of legal, cooking up a fake rap sheet and linking it to a string of particularly gruesome, unsolved murders. Crow's creation is nothing short of a monster—a bloodthirsty assassin who you'd believe capable of the most heinous acts. She's so confident in her 'deadly skills' that she won't take a dime until the job's done, turning down any upfront payment.

"He's in," Shelly exhales, her fist tightening in some kind of victory pump—as if my life isn't dangling by a thread.

Seeing it on the screen makes it even more real. Tomorrow, at Eva's funeral, a hitwoman, supposedly on Roman Knox's payroll, will be gunning for me.

"I can't wait to watch you take out that bitch," writes Knox.

"It's the break we've been waiting for," Shelly says, all business. "I'll tap my contacts—it'll be squeaky clean. A tight crew, six or seven max, bypassing this station to nix any leaks. When he makes his move, we'll have him."

"Besides, Chief Davis would never sign off on this," I argue.

"Don't sweat it. I'm not gonna shoot you," Crow quips, all sarcasm. "I'll be right by your side, promise."

But I can't help the lump in my throat when I remind them, "There's no telling if he's hired more than one shooter." My own words taste like fear as I swallow them down.

***

Standing in front of the mirror the following day, wrestling into my black funeral suit, feels like arming for battle. The twelve millimeters of my level IIIA bulletproof vest promise a fighting chance against a .44 Magnum or light assault rifles—if there's a backup shooter in the crowd. But my head? That's a different story. It's gonna be a bullseye if Roman hired a marksman worth their salt.

Just out of the shower, the irony hit me hard. We're off to Eva's funeral to pay respects to another of Roman Knox's casualties, and I could be the next headline.

"Damn, you look killer in that black dress," I let out a sigh when Crow emerges from the bathroom, her dark hair still dripping.

"Could say the same for you, but those bags under your eyes are a dead giveaway," she teases with a smirk.

"Oh, great," I grumble, "just stop short of saying the vest makes me look fat."

"I need to tell you something, just in case..." her voice trails off, and she pauses, biting her lip, struggling to meet my eyes. The morning's been rough on both of us.

"Just in case...?" I prompt, my heart hammering.

She exhales long and hard, then her gaze flickers. "In case things go south today... you need to know that I—" She stops again, a hand nervously raking her neck, fighting for the words.

Crow's vulnerability splits me open.

"It's not gonna come to that, Angie. We'll get through this and nail that bastard. Couple of hours, and we'll be toasting to victory," I assure her, squeezing her hand in mine—more to steady my own nerves.

"These past weeks with you, Izzy... they've been incredible. Never thought I could feel this way, not with my past," she shakes her head, her blue eyes glistening.

"Stop, you're gonna make me cry," I plead, resting my forehead against hers.

What she's trying to say is clear as day, even if the words stick in her throat.

"I'm falling for you. The thought of a future without us together, it scares the hell out of me, Izzy... I—damn it... I love you," Crow finally admits, and her words knock the wind out of me.

"Come here," I whisper, pulling her into a kiss.

Her lips part softly, an unspoken invitation. Crow's eyes flutter shut as my hand caresses her cheek, savoring the moment. It's a tender, sweet kiss, a vow for a life together.

"Should've said it sooner," she jokes when we break apart.

Before I can respond, I cling to her like she's my lifeline, afraid to let go. I bury my face in her neck, inhaling her scent, wishing time would just stop. And in her embrace, just for a second, I forget that in an hour, I'll face the toughest moment of my life.

Chapter 26

Crow

As we step into the cemetery for Eva's funeral, the air crackles with an unspoken tension. I'm squinting through dark shades, scanning the place. Shelly's handpicked agents blend in with the crowd, their presence a silent dance of stealth and normalcy.

"They really shouldn't be here," I mutter, my voice barely a whisper. "Davis will have our heads if he catches wind of this." A covert op with a cop as bait—it's insane. But it's so insane Roman won't see it coming.

Isabella squeezes my hand, her skin a contrast to the cold bite in the air. The space around Eva's grave fills up, and I'm silently pleading that Roman didn't plan for a plan B hitman.

"Stay calm, stick with Izzy, focus on the funeral," Shelly's words echo in my head. Trust is a luxury I can't afford, not with Isabella's life on the line. The thought of losing her tightens my chest like a vice.

Despite her brave front, I know Izzy's scared. I give her hand a reassuring squeeze and force a smile. "We got this," I say, trying to believe it myself. Roman's mind is a twisted maze; you never know where it'll turn.

My gaze catches on the casket, a sharp pain lancing through me. A blond guy lounges against a tree in the distance, a potential threat in every line of his posture. I tap my earpiece hidden in my hair—three rapid taps. Shelly's team is on alert. Two taps back. False alarm. He's just another mourner.

The service starts, and Isabella turns her head, her eyes searching for reassurance. She's the one in the crosshairs today.

Then, there he is, emerging from behind a stark white headstone—a broad man in a cap, trying to hide a tattoo that marks him. Roman Knox.

My hand flies to my earpiece—three firm taps. Agents scan the perimeter, each one tapping their mic in succession. I can almost taste the adrenaline; Shelly's signal will unleash them on Roman. Simple, clean, over in seconds—or so we hope.

But as any good street-raised girl knows, plans have a funny way of going sideways when you least expect it.

The priest's prayer echoes through the cemetery's silence, punctuated by the occasional sniffle. I sneak a glance at Roman and feel a twist of unease. He's not reacting to the agents swarming him. Hands up, behind his head, he kneels, head bowed in mock reverence.

Something's off.

Then it happens.

A gunshot shatters the calm. Chaos erupts. People scatter, some hitting the dirt. Screams blend with prayers behind tombstones. Isabella's face drains of color next to me. She crumples to her knees, a broken doll. Another shot, and her blood sprays across my face as I catch her.

"Izzy," she whispers, eyes wide with terror, locking onto mine.

The shooter fires off more rounds, probably with agents hot on his trail, but I'm not even checking to see if they've got him. Nor do I look to see if Roman's slipped away in the bedlam. My world narrows to her.

"Please, Izzy... stay with me, you'll be okay," I choke out.

I'm aiming for calm, don't want to scare her more than she already is, but her white blouse soaks up blood, blooming with cruel red flowers. Her eyes flutter closed, and she goes limp in my arms.

"Izzy, look at me! Look at me!" I scream.

It's a raw, gut-wrenching cry. Pure desperation. Agony.

Chapter 27

Crow

Everything blurs, a thick fog of confusion wrapping around us. The coppery stench of blood smears my hands; screams and panic slice through the air.

Sirens wail in the distance, growing louder. Before I can even brace myself, paramedics swarm Isabella, while one grabs me, insisting I step back to let them work.

Their words are a jumbled rush.

"She's lost a lot of blood."

"We need to check for a brachial artery hit."

"Transfusion, gotta prevent hypovolemic shock."

"O negative, let's move."

They're like a well-oiled machine, slapping a cervical collar on her and hoisting her onto a stretcher. I stumble after them, dazed, eyes glued to Isabella's still form.

"You can't ride in the ambulance," one medic says, firm.

I shoot back with a shaky threat, "Try and stop me, and I'll rip your damn head off."

"Just let her," another one snaps. "We're in a hurry!"

The ride to the hospital is torture. My gaze flicks from Isabella to the cardiac monitor, clinging to each beep as if it's a lifeline.

"Please," I beg, swiping tears from my cheeks, "you have to save her."

The medic who let me ride with them leans close, a comforting hand on my shoulder, and gives me a squeeze. She offers a smile. "She'll be okay. The vest caught the bullet. Probably some busted ribs, sure, but it hit a lucky spot. Lost a lot of blood, though, because of the second shot. The arm wound's under control now, looks clean." Her words are hopeful, but the reddening bandage doesn't inspire confidence.

"Long as those ribs didn't splinter and puncture something important," the EMT—who was so adamant about not letting me in the ambulance—murmurs. I swear, I'm going to give his computer a virus so epic that it'll have its own biography.

Once we hit the hospital, it's like a scene from a TV series: all hustle and scrubs swarming the gurney. They whisk Isabella through sterile, steel doors, and just like that, she's gone from my sight.

I'm shivering in the waiting room, haunted by the memory of her eyes, wide and terrified, Isabella mouthing my name before blacking out. That's the stuff of nightmares, right there.

The clock is the real enemy now, ticking away with this torturous lethargy, like it's in on the whole ordeal. I'm fighting the image of Izzy on an operating table, still and pale.

Then, out of nowhere, a nurse is shouting my name. I sprint to her, "Tell me something, anything," but she's either clueless or handcuffed by protocol. A doctor finally approaches.

"How is she? Please," I beg through a damn waterfall on my face.

He smiles, weary but reassuring, "Calm down, she's going to be fine," and damn if those aren't the most beautiful words I've ever heard.

"So, she's okay?" I need to hear it again, just to make sure.

"Surprisingly well. She's tough. We stitched up her arm; she'll have a pretty badass scar, though. No nerve damage and the vest took the chest hit. She'll be sore, but there's no internal injuries," he explains.

I nearly collapse with relief and, like a zombie, they guide me on wobbly legs to Isabella's room.

"Your girlfriend's here," a nurse by her side says, with a hint of annoyance. "Goodness, she's got a temper! Tried to throw a punch at one of our EMTs and cursed out everyone because we wouldn't let her into surgery with you."

"Hey, how are you feeling?" I say, sidling up to her, pushing the nurse's probably-exaggerated tales out of my mind—though, to be fair, I barely remember anything from the ambulance ride.

"Everything hurts, but good," she tries a smile, and it's like the sun after a storm.

"Good thing our hitman's aim sucked," I quip with a smirk.

Izzy smiles, and as she instinctively reaches out with her right arm, pain flashes across her face.

"Stay put, rest up. Damn, you scared the hell out of me. Thought I'd lost you for good," I confess, leaning in to kiss her forehead.

"Did they catch them?"

"I don't know, Izzy. No word from Shelly. It was a freaking mess out there, and all I could think about was keeping you in my arms," I apologize.

"You know what's crazy? The last thing I saw before blacking out was your face. Kinda weird, but I thought if I was gonna die, that wasn't a bad last view—even with your eyes all teary."

"You were probably in shock. I've seen my fair share of shootouts on the streets," I say, trying to keep it tough.

"You were crying, which was, I gotta say, super sweet."

"Damn it, Izzy, you're such an idiot. I thought you were dying."

"It's okay. I like seeing you get all misty-eyed now and then. Let's keep it between us," she whispers, winking through the pain.

"A flood of tears, not just misty-eyed," I admit, rolling my eyes. "Seeing all that blood... damn, Izzy. I've never been so scared in my life. I can't lose you. I love you too much."

"Can you say that again?"

"I love you, you fool."

Just as she opens her mouth to reply, my phone buzzes and my heart skips seeing who's calling.

Shelly.

"How's Alvarez?" she greets.

"Too chipper; must be the drugs they've got her on. Please tell me you caught those bastards."

"Don't you trust me? We got 'em!"

I let out a long sigh of relief and hug Isabella, who winces a bit. I can almost picture Shelly, fist-pumping in victory.

"Tell her I want to do the questioning," Izzy grunts.

Shelly's already off the line, explaining how they tracked down Roman's operation from his phone records.

"You should see this place. It's loaded with evidence. Call logs, encrypted emails, financials, photos. You wouldn't believe it. It'll take time to crack all his security, but we've got him nailed. He's going away for life," she assures me. "Guy was so full of himself, documented everything. I've never seen someone so self-absorbed."

"He'll have plenty of time for push-ups now."

"How are you holding up?" she cuts in.

"Me? Fine. A little shootout's nothing."

"Yeah, right," she jokes, but even without seeing her, I know she's not buying it.

Chapter 28

Crow

"What's it like being on the other side of the looking glass, Crow?" Shelly teases.

Honestly, it's weird watching the interrogation from behind the one-way mirror. I always wondered what it was like over here. This side's way more chill. Cops hang back, sipping coffee, not barking like they do in the hot seat.

Izzy, well, she's stubborn as hell. With her right arm all slung up so she can't move it, she's dead set on running the show. She's taken this whole mess super personal, and I'm not sure Chief Davis is on board with that.

Isabella sits across from Roman, who, despite staring down the barrel of life behind bars, is oozing arrogance. Cuffed and cornered, but still playing untouchable.

"Detective, did you have a little accident?" Roman pokes, trying to rattle her, but lucky for us, Izzy doesn't bite.

"Let's start with the easy stuff, Roman," Isabella fires back, pinning him with her gaze. "We know you paid a guy named Jeremy Bennett to plant bombs in Marla Trenton's apartment."

"Why on earth would I do that?" Roman drawls, eyeing his nails with a bored air of indifference. His lawyer gives him a nod like he's acing it.

"Cyber crimes has cracked a chunk of your files. It's totally pointless to keep up your denials. You've gotta be real full of yourself to keep evidence around, encrypted or not. It'll take us time, but we'll get to all of it. You're done. You know it. It'll be way worse for you if you don't play ball," Izzy warns him.

Roman Knox's facade is hanging by a thread, but it's his lawyer whose face is a picture show of dread. From behind the glass, you see everything clear as day.

"Is this all about your brother Caleb?" Isabella presses.

The mention of his brother's name, and Roman's face tells a whole new story.

"He died because of that bitch," he snarls with a rage that feels like a slap to the face.

"Shouldn't you be mad at the ones who actually killed him? Last I checked, Angie was in a whole different prison, miles away from Caleb."

171

"Angie?" he scoffs with such venom I can almost taste it. "That woman's a curse. Everything she touches turns to disaster. I bet you love her keeping your bed warm at night, but just wait. She's trouble, like a damn magnet. She'll wreck your life, detective," and I feel a chill run down my spine at his words; they're meant to cut deep.

"Don't listen to him," Shelly whispers, her arm snaking around my waist, her touch grounding me against the sting of his words.

Roman's gaze pierces through the one-way mirror, and for a split second, I'm convinced he can actually see us, and I shiver.

"Caleb's dead because of you, bitch," he accuses, staring right at the mirror. "Does your detective girlfriend know? Have you told her about your little side gig of framing people?"

"So, all this... three murders, two attempted, hiring hitmen off the Dark Web... this is all for revenge on Crow?" Isabella cuts in, and I can't help but release the breath I didn't realize I was holding.

Roman just smiles, with no hint of remorse. To him, those lives are no more than bugs squashed under his shoe, a display of his power, deciding who lives and who dies. He's always been off, but now, I'm convinced he's totally lost it.

"You know you're screwed, right?" Isabella mutters, leaning in closer to him.

"I know," he admits.

"Good, now let's talk about the mole in the precinct. It's clear some-one's been feeding you details from the investigation. Help us out with this, and I'll see you don't end up in the worst hellhole in the States."

"Jesus, you haven't figured it out yet, detective?" His tone is icy, mocking. It's all a game to him, and he thinks he's winning.

"Give me a name," Isabella demands.

"Who do you think, detective? Who else hates Crow just as much as I do? For the same reason." He taunts.

"Enlighten me," Izzy shoots back, her voice steady, but I can tell she's on edge.

Roman leans back in his chair, hands cradling his neck, a smirk of pride playing on his lips. "You'd think those cybercrime department folks would have cracked it by now. Really, I'm surprised they haven't, considering how weak the encryption is on those emails with that... woman. Never liked her; she had this air about her, like she thought she was above us all. Told my brother plenty of times, but did he listen? Nope, just kept on seeing her."

Izzy snaps, irritation clear in her voice, "Can we focus, please?"

"Right, Dana Kalinsky," Roman mutters under his breath.

"Kalinsky? What's she got to do with Crow or your brother Caleb?"

He can't help but let a chuckle slip, "Oh, detective, seems like this station's got more secrets than the CIA. And speaking of secrets, do your buddies here know you're sleeping with Crow?"

"Stay on topic!"

"Kalinsky was secretly seeing my brother. Thought she was too good to go public with it. When Caleb ended up dead in jail, she was out for blood. Me? I just fanned the flames, used her hate. Wish I hadn't, though. She should've tipped me off about the funeral being a setup. Risky move, Crow, but clever!" His voice drips with sarcasm as he addresses me through the one-way glass.

"Fuck, Kalinsky," I whisper, shaking my head in disbelief.

In a flash, Isabella storms out of the interrogation room and into ours, her command is swift and decisive, "Don't let her leave the building, but don't make a move. I want to be the one to cuff her."

"This isn't over, you know that, right, Crow?" Roman taunts. "Eight years behind bars, you know news travels, even from one prison to another. The Calderóns will be thrilled to find out who snitched."

"You're just talking," Isabella cuts him off, "It wasn't Crow."

"Maybe, but I don't need proof. Didn't need it to take down my brother, did they? Your girlfriend's not safe, inside jail or out. And just a heads-up, death follows her. She's a harbinger of doom,"

***

"Wow, that was... intense," I quip as Isabella strides into our room, her interrogation skills still giving me the kind of chill that makes you want to check your own alibi. "Almost makes a person want to wet themselves."

"It's over. We've got enough to put him away for life," Isabella assures me, leaning in for a kiss that catches me, and a couple of her colleagues, off-guard. "Now, let's go get Kalinsky," she says with a smile that could light up the darkest corners of any police station.

"Heh, I was about to say, 'I told you so about Kalinsky, and you blew me off,' but that kiss just earned you a get-out-of-jail-free card," I joke, following her through the station's buzzing corridors.

Isabella doesn't just open Dana Kalinsky's office door—she kicks it in. Dana bolts upright from her chair, her face a picture painted with shock and fury.

"What the hell are you doing? Have you lost your mind?" Kalinsky screams.

"You're under arrest," Izzy growls. "You have the right to—"

"Spare me the Miranda rights; I know them by heart. What is all this shit about?"

"It's over, Kalinsky. Roman Knox ratted you out. We've got proof of your little chats," Izzy declares, her grin betraying the sweet taste of victory.

Kalinky's face runs through a palette of colors, from ghostly pale to an alarming shade of red as the accusation sinks in. She opens her mouth as if words should be pouring out, but silence reigns, her jaw just hanging there as they slap the cuffs on.

"Yeah? You're pretty smug with your street rat sweetheart," she spits at Izzy. "I felt the same about Caleb. I really hope your love story ends the same way, with that bitch dying in jail, bleeding out in the bathroom without a soul to care."

***

"Holy shit, remind me never to tick you off. You're terrifying when you're on a roll," I jest as we enter her apartment.

Isabella closes her eyes, a smirk playing on her lips, shaking her head in disbelief. "I just wanted to wrap this whole thing up," she whispers, collapsing onto the couch and motioning for me to join her.

"Same here," I confirm, straddling her thighs with a comfortable ease.

For a long moment, we're silent, but sometimes silence speaks louder than words. Her gaze and the kiss that follows tell me everything. And when she murmurs, "Stay by my side forever," I melt, utterly and completely.

"Are you crying?" she asks, lifting my chin with her fingers.

"Shut up, idiot," I sigh, peppering her neck with kisses.

Resting my head on her shoulder, our fingers intertwined, I'm content. I lift my gaze, our eyes lock, and I steal a quick kiss, earning a smile from her that's all the sunshine I need.

I know there'll be challenges, loose ends from a thorny past, but we'll face them together.

The black roses that once bound us have blossomed into something beautiful. A future that the street kid in me would never have dared to dream of.

Other Books by the Same Author

If you liked this book, you'll probably like the following books as well:

Trilogy Watson Memorial Hospital

Interconnected stand-alone books

Doctor Stone: A Sapphic Medical Romance

A decade ago, a tragic surgery forever altered the lives of Dr. Jackie Stone and Sarah Taylor. Haunted by the loss of that patient, Dr. Stone has since immersed herself in her work, believing that if she stays busy, she can escape the pain of her past.

Sarah Taylor, now a determined intern at Manhattan's prestigious Watson Memorial Hospital, finds herself under the supervision of the very doctor who was present during her brother's ill-fated surgery ten years ago.

As she strives to become a renowned surgeon, Sarah must grapple with the emotional weight of working in the same hospital where her brother died, under the watchful eye of the woman who couldn't save him.

Don't miss this riveting sapphic medical romance exploring the intricate dance of forgiveness, healing, and the transformative power of love.

Doctor Torres: A Sapphic Medical Romance

At 27, Nicole Hunt is a rising star in health and wellness, captivating audiences with her dynamic podcast and entertaining Tik-Tok presence. In a special series for Heart Month, she sets her sights on interviewing some of the nation's most prominent medical professionals, including the reclusive Dr. Inés Torres.

Dr. Torres is a 40-year-old distinguished cardiologist with a reputation as steely as the scalpel she wields. Her life revolves entirely around her work, leaving no room for love or leisure.

As the effervescent Nicole steps into Dr. Torres's strictly regimented world, sparks fly, and an unexpected connection forms between the two women. Can Nicole's warmth and charisma melt Dr. Torres's icy exterior and unlock the door to a new, fulfilling chapter in her life?

Immerse yourself in this captivating sapphic medical romance, a heartwarming journey of love, healing, and the power of letting go.

Doctor Harris: A Sapphic Medical Romance

A doctor in love with a resident.

A resident in love with a patient.

A patient in love with herself.

Dr. Rachel Harris has always played by the book, until a mysterious woman arrives at the hospital after a grave accident, sending her world into a tailspin.

As the patient lies in an induced coma, Dr. Harris finds solace in her daydreams, crafting an enchanting romance with this enigmatic woman. Her fantasies provide an escape from her otherwise regimented life, stirring feelings she's never experienced before.

However, reality comes crashing down when the patient finally awakens, revealing herself to be a moody, self-absorbed woman who bears no resemblance to the person Rachel had come to love in her mind. As Dr. Harris grapples with her unexpected feelings, she must confront the blurred lines between fantasy and reality, desire and responsibility.

Don't miss this mesmerizing sapphic medical romance that delves into the complexities of love, self-discovery, and the journey of personal growth.

***

Under a Shooting Star

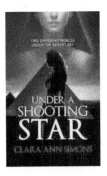

A Hollywood star in the midst of a career downturn.

A Bedouin guide deeply rooted in the traditions of her people.

Two different worlds under the desert sky.

Victoria Iverson has everything fame can buy. Yet, as the years stack up, her life begins to feel devoid of meaning.

Her latest film role takes her to the endless dunes of the Sinai desert. There, she'll meet Istar, her enigmatic Bedawi guide.

Against the backdrop of the desert, their lives intertwine in ways neither could have imagined.

But is it enough to shatter the high walls dividing their cultures?

The Missing Letters of Sara Nelson: A Second Chance Sapphic Romance

At 42, Samantha Thomson's picture-perfect life is crumbling. Fresh from a painful divorce, she's struggling to raise two teenage daughters while trudging through a monotonous routine.

Her childhood friend Olivia Mitchell lives life on the edge. While filming her documentaries, Olivia has spent over two decades traveling the globe and fighting for justice.

When their paths cross again, long-buried feelings ignite.

And when Samantha discovers twelve romantic WWII love letters hidden in an old book, they spark an unexpected thirst for adventure.

Spurred by Olivia, both women journey through snow-covered Vermont villages to deliver the long-lost letters.

Along the way, both women must confront their own ghosts. Can righting the wrongs of the past inspire them to live boldly again?

Join Samantha and Olivia on an uplifting voyage of second chances, reminding us it's never too late to start living.

Crossed Destinies: A Sapphic Billionaire Romance

The CEO of a technology company whose methods border the limits of ethics.

A journalist in search of the truth and eager to prove herself.

What can go wrong?

From their first encounter, an undeniable chemistry draws them together. Yet, their professional ambitions threaten to drive a wedge between them.

As Sarah digs deeper into the inner workings of Hailey's empire, she uncovers shocking secrets that threaten to expose the dark underbelly behind its success. Torn between protecting the woman she's falling for and revealing the truth, Sarah grapples with the biggest decision of her life.

Will she prioritize her commitment to journalistic integrity and unveil the truth, or will her deepening feelings for Hailey cloud her judgment?

Can her relationship survive the pressure, or will it blow up?

Passions flare, and ethical lines blur in this tension-filled romance set in the high-stakes world of corporate finance. When matters of the heart collide with the quest for truth, the fallout could destroy careers, relationships, and even lives.

Tie Break: A Sapphic Sports Romance

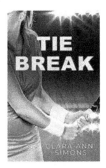

Brooke McKlain is a household name for tennis fans.

Elena has no idea who she is. She just knows she's ruining her life.

When Brooke decides to take a much-needed break at a luxury hotel in Hawaii, she doesn't expect that the woman who challenged her from the very first moment will show her what love is.

Elena will make her question many things, and now love spins onto her court, revealing what she's been missing.

But their worlds are too different, and things are never as easy as they seem... especially when the public image you want to give outweighs your feelings.

YOUNG ADULT SAPPHIC ROMANCE

Liar: A Young Adult "fake date" LGBTQ+ Romance

Nina Álvarez is living the dream.

She's the high school basketball team captain, a social media sensation, and one of the most popular girls at school. But when a misplaced comment goes viral, Nina's future comes crashing down.

With accusations of homophobia threatening to destroy everything she's worked for, Nina devises a daring plan: fake-date Alexia Taylor, a proud and openly gay girl from her high school.

Alexia is her polar opposite. She's a brilliant, introverted aspiring scientist with her sights set on NASA. And she wants nothing to do with Nina's scheme.

However, when Alexia's best friend Cris gets involved, she soon finds herself unable to say no.

As Nina and Alexia play their roles in this high-stakes game of pretend, they find themselves drawn to each other in ways they never expected. Amidst the whirlwind of high school drama, basketball games, and social media scandals, the two girls discover that sometimes, the line between love and lies isn't so clear.

Operation Vanessa

Riley, the high school resident rebel, never thought she'd fall for anyone—especially not Vanessa, the untouchable cheerleading squad captain.

In a world where social expectations and invisible barriers dictate the rules, they are on opposite sides of the high school spectrum.

But love won't be ignored. Overwhelmed by her feelings, Riley turns to Alexia, a straight-A student with a gift for words. Together, they hatch a daring plan inspired by Cyrano de Bergerac to capture the cheerleader's heart.